Twelve Golden Threads

Twelve Golden Threads

Lessons for Successful Living from Grama's Quilt

Aliske Webb

HarperCollins*Publishers*

Designed by Nancy Singer

ISBN 0–06–017463–3

To Michael
for deep oceans of love
mountains of encouragement
wide meadows of sunshine optimism
and still forests of tranquillity

CONTENTS

Contents

INTRODUCTION

*I*f you are lucky, you have a quilt that was passed down to you from a grandmother or even a great-grandmother. And with the quilt you have the family's story embroidered around it. The delicate stitches bind you together with your sisters, aunts, mothers, and all your foremothers, into a complex pattern of love and creativity. You can wrap yourself in its comfort and history, knowing that what was passed on to you, will be passed on again. From woman to woman.

My paternal grandmother was about as poor as everyone was in "those days." Her quilt is simple, imperfect, inelegant. And precious. Once I broke off an engagement with a man because I returned home to find him asleep on my couch with his shoes on, on Grama's quilt. Petty you say. But such irreverence for things that are important to me was an evocative symbol of a relationship already going wrong.

Grandmother's quilt hangs in my sewing room to inspire me—to connect me. Tradition is not only what comes to us from before, created in the past. It is also what we newly create to become the inheritance of future generations, who will talk about us in their turn. We come from an unseen past and move on to an unknown future—from love into hope.

Studying our quilts, we discover the fibers that weave us all together—a fabric of connections—some random, some determined. Our fingers trace the stitches, our eyes wander and caress the faded colors, the wrinkled design, the time-worn frayed edges. And our minds linger in memory. Memories that are both our own and that have been handed down to us, like the most fragile, cherished heirloom.

We have a view of our grandmother as a woman who sat peaceably by a cozy fire through long winter months, stitching away with love in her heart and a centeredness in her soul. Her truth may be something else entirely, but it is a warm, comforting image because her quilt gives us a warm, comfortable feeling. What we think of as the "good old days" were known then as "these trying times." Likewise, it is hard to imagine future generations being nostalgic about our own turbulent "now."

Our romance of the past is always of a simpler place, a slower pace, an easier time, because we visit it only in our minds. Like well-washed calico, history fades reality. When we envision our pioneer grandmothers, we don't actually feel their reality. We don't experience their drafty, damp rooms. Our bodies don't ache from their day-long labors of washing, cooking, cleaning, gardening, and child-tending that started before dawn and ended well after dark. Our shoulders and arms and fingers aren't cramped from hours of mending, sewing, and knitting—all done by hand, without machinery—by dim and unreliable light. We don't feel their illnesses, headaches, worries, fatigue. We are distanced from their pain.

Pain is always personal and separates people. Yet we can share the joy of others. Joy unites. Our grandmothers' quilting was a natural part of their lives, done from necessity and love. Their joy in creativity raised it to a higher level, and we are lucky to be graced by their spiritual inheritance. Joy transcends time and space. We respond across the years and distance like an untouched harp string reverberating in tune with another plucked string across a still room.

We are often awed by our pioneer grandmothers' force of character. They forbore a physical life that would daunt the strongest of us today, a life that would bore most of us. Yes, they lacked our choices and the freedom that too often leaves us feeling disoriented and unfulfilled. We admire those pioneers' sense of place, of who they were, and their belief that what they did mattered. We envy their connected-ness to their families, their world, their communities, themselves.

When I touch an old quilt, I know it is affirming that even from exhaustion, hardship, little if any acknowledgment or reward, can come a body of work that not only serves its useful purpose but that is fresh, creative, beautiful—and spiritually undaunted. Here is a celebration of work, and ultimately, of Life.

We are daughters of that tradition. How can we do less?

OCTOBER

A Visit to Grama

$\mathcal{F}$ollowing a business degree at college and after several months looking for work, Jennifer, my eldest daughter, was offered a job with a bank in their Investment Services division. So today she was bursting with energy and couldn't wait to tell Grama the terrific news. She wants to be a stockbroker and make a million dollars. This is really "it" for her.

Grama, actually her paternal grandmother, is nearly eighty-five and lives in Clareville, in an apartment in a seniors' complex. The facility has everything from small individual apartments where seniors can look after themselves and maintain their privacy and independence, to extended-care units where residents can receive increasing levels of physical and medical assistance. Although the hallways are painted an old institutional dull green, inside Grama's apartment her decor is warm and inviting. It's full of overstuffed chintz-covered chairs and a lifetime of mementos.

Grama has many friends throughout the complex. She's been there for almost twenty years. "Longer than a prison sentence for murder," she cheerfully reminds us. The residence was the best that her pension and my late husband, Jack, and his family could afford at the time. So even though we could now move her someplace much roomier and fancier, she is happy with her home and won't budge. Did I mention she was stubborn? You bet. I'm sure the angels have come for her several times but she just wouldn't go.

So once a month we, also stubbornly, drive all the way to visit her. Did that "all the way" sound like a burden? It isn't. I simply mean that it's too far to pop in for tea. Our visits often seem like the mad tea parties in *Alice in Wonderland*, full of laughter and good woman-talk about the important things in life like shoe sales, hairdos, the Amazon rainforest, and black holes in space. It's how the three generations of women in our family stay connected, share good news and bad news, and try to make sense of the world around us.

Jennifer, Susan, my youngest daughter, and I drive to see Grama. Son Robbie is out west this year studying oceanography. The one joy I have in his absence is that I no longer unexpectedly find incredibly ugly, invariably wet creatures in my bathroom— or worse, in jars in the refrigerator. This has been a long-term forbearance, I assure you.

One high school year on the East Coast, Robbie won an astonishing first prize for his science project—wherein he set out to prove that everything from the sea, or at least in our bay, was edible. He systematically brought home, dissected, cooked, and ate, what seemed to be an entire zoophyllum. Much to the disgusted squeals of the girls, who naturally couldn't resist watching. I think he chose a West Coast college simply to see if everything in the western waters tastes any different.

Jack always joked that Robbie would end up a chef in a seafood restaurant, but for the customers' sake he hoped he didn't. I tell you this aside to give you some idea of what the men in this family are like. We miss them.

When we arrived in Clareville this morning, Grama was finishing another quilt, sewing on the binding around the edges. This particular quilt is a deep blue-and-red eight-pointed Ohio Star pattern. It takes Grama nearly a year to complete each quilt by hand. Years ago we bought her a sewing machine but she would only use it for dressmaking and repairs. Her quilts are all handsewn, with fine neat stitches. She has had a lot of practice. Her eyes are weaker and her fingers are stiffer, so instead of compromising the work, she simply slowed her pace.

"Oh, Grama! What a beautiful quilt!" Susan enthused, as Grama tied the thread in a knot and then smoothed the quilt out for us to see. Susan gathered it up.

"Can I?" she asked, as she wrapped the down-like material around her.

"It's lovely," admired Jennifer.

"It's so soft," Susan marveled. "Even more than usual."

"I made it from old flannel pajamas and backed it with old flannelette sheets. It's for Mr. Fulton upstairs. He has a skin problem you know, and he needed it extra soft. I wanted to make it as cuddly as a baby blanket," Grama explained as she stepped to the kitchen to make a pot of our favorite Earl Grey tea.

Grama has given many of her quilts to people in the home. There are more than twenty bodies who sleep peacefully and dream colorfully under her quilts. Most were complete strangers to her when Grama perceived there was a need for warmth, comfort, or cheery color, and there she would be at the stranger's door, making a new friend. And of course, many quilts have been passed gently back to Grama when her friends died. But for her there would always be a new door to take it to, a new friend to make.

"Do you ever wonder how many quilts you've made, Grama?" I asked.

"All together, I guess hundreds if you count all the quilting bees we used to have back on the farm. All the neighboring women would work hard every winter to make pretty new quilt tops so we could get together in the spring and start quilting. Everyone would work on one quilt and that way we would finish faster. So you could say I made hundreds by working on the other women's quilts. And they worked on mine too, of course."

"Must have been quite a party," said Jennifer. "All those women sewing and carrying on."

"Remember, we didn't have television in those days, and we were eager to visit and talk. We laughed a lot," Grama remembered fondly while she set out fancy teacups and a plate of gingersnaps.

"What did the men think of you women partying it up like that?" Susan asked reaching for a cookie.

"Well, that's why we called them bees, so we could be busy as bees and productive in the final report. But if the men were around, we were as quiet as mice so they wouldn't find out how much fun we were having," whispered Grama in a low conspiratorial voice.

"Hmmm," said Jennifer, about to make one of her twenty-one-year-old feminist pronouncements. But she was sideswiped by humor as we all looked at

Grama and pictured her and her pussycat friends pretending to be mice. We broke out laughing—at the truth of men in those times and the conspiracy of women at all times.

"Now, Jen, tell me about your new job," commanded Grama, as she patted away her sewing things to pay full attention to the bright young woman beside her.

For several minutes Jennifer warbled on in detail about her news, her eyes dancing with excitement and promise. Her cup of tea grew cold as it sat forgotten on the end table beside her.

"And by the time I'm thirty, I'll be a millionaire and buy a ranch in Colorado," she said with final conviction.

"Whoa, girl! How did we get from 'I start on Monday' to Colorado so fast?" I asked.

"I am going to be successful. You'll see," she asserted again.

Grama laughed, "Oh, I'm sure you will do it, honey. If you believe it and want it enough, you can do anything you set your mind to."

"See, Grama believes me," defended Jennifer petulantly.

"Grama believes in you. And so do I. We know you can do whatever you want. As I've always said, if you believe you can, you can. If you believe you cannot, you cannot. Either way, you will be right. Belief in yourself is where you must start. But let's not go

6

flying off the handle. You know, like the guy who 'jumped on his horse and rode off in all directions.'"

I sighed inwardly, hearing myself in my all too familiar admonishing-mother role. Even when I don't have my hands on my hips, it sounds like I do.

"Look, we all know that having a goal, or goals, is one of the most important things in life. And the first step is to have an enthusiastic attitude of desire and belief. Okay, so you jumped on the horse of enthusiasm. Now, you have to train it to go where you want it to go."

"Some people think it is easier to simply ride a horse in the direction it is already going," Grama put in mischievously and grinned, then added seriously, "but of course that way you don't necessarily get to where you want to go. Your mom is right, Jen. What she means by 'train the horse' is you have to develop the appropriate habits that will help you become the kind of successful person you want to be, and achieve the things you want to do."

"Like 'riding habits'?" Jennifer joked.

Grama chuckled at the pun and continued, "We all have habits, dozens of them. We don't even think about them. That is why they are important to us. It means that we don't have to consciously think about every little detail of our life. Some of our habits are good, some are bad. Why not make your habits work to your advantage whenever possible?"

"What do you mean?" Jennifer asked.

"There are two kinds of habits," I interjected. "Attitude habits are how you usually think and feel. Action habits are how you behave. They are interconnected. Remember the action-reaction law in your physics class, which states that for every action there is an equal and opposite reaction? Well, everything you do produces a result, and every result affects everything you do."

"Like a feedback loop," Jennifer nodded.

"Right. Habits are simply the daily manifestation of your character and your values. Who you are inside creates what you do, and what you do reinforces who you are. That way habits, and character, become stronger. Character creates actions and actions reinforce character," I said.

"But wait a minute. Let's go back a step, Jen. I would like to know what you mean by 'be successful'?" Grama asked.

"Well, first of all I want an exciting job. Then I want a big house, a new car, and lots of great clothes to wear. I want to travel, to go to Paris. You know, everything!" Jennifer enthused.

"Why do you want these things? What do they mean to you?" Grama pursued.

"Well, a good job means having enough money to do whatever I want. I guess ultimately it means freedom. You know, like they say in those lottery commercials on television. A beautiful house would sure impress my friends. Nice clothes just make me feel good. Is that wrong?" Jennifer started to sound suspicious.

"Not at all," Grama reassured her. "So what you're saying is those things are just ways to satisfy needs, such as feeling good or impressing your friends. Are there other ways to feel good, besides through money or material things?" Grama asked.

"Sure, Grama. Okay, I know it isn't the money itself, necessarily. It's just that people accept money as a symbol of a successful person. You're not going to give me that old saw 'money won't buy happiness' or 'money is evil,' are you?" she objected.

"No, my budding capitalist," I promised. I looked at Grama for help.

She just smiled sagely, shrugged her shoulders, and said to me, "Some roads are longer than others."

Then she turned to Jennifer and asked, "Jen, did you do well in high school?"

"Yes, of course, Grama, you know I did," she replied.

"Were you successful?"

"Yes, but that was different."

"How?"

"Because my goal was to get the best grades so I could get into a good college," Jennifer explained.

"Which you did. Were you successful at college?" Grama asked.

"Yes, but that was different again," she answered.

"How?"

"Because my goal then was to land a good job when I graduated college," she defended. "It's only out working that I can have any real success. School was just practice."

"Jen, honey, nothing is 'just practice.' It's all for real. Life is not a dress rehearsal," Grama admonished her gently. "In any event, you were successful, or felt successful, at different times for different reasons, relative to your goal at that time. Is it possible perhaps that success is measured by different criteria at different times of your life? And acquiring things may be just one of many ways to measure success?" Grama concluded.

"Okay. I get it. You want me to rethink what success means to me. But I really do want all those things, Grama, and I don't see why I shouldn't want them." She started to pout.

"We aren't saying that you shouldn't want, or have, all the wonderful things there are in life to enjoy," I explained. "We just want you to think it through carefully and know what success is to you, not what others measure it by. What you think is important may not be what others think is important. Just be aware of all your options before you exercise your choice and set goals that represent success to you." I let it rest.

"Do you know how to be successful?" Grama took another tack.

"No. Not yet. But I'm going to learn," Jennifer asserted.

"Good. That's the right attitude. If you want something strongly enough, and you are willing to do whatever it takes, and in this case you are willing to learn, then you will succeed," Grama advised her.

"That sounds reasonable to me," Jennifer agreed.

"Then maybe the first thing you might want to learn is about success itself," Grama suggested slyly.

"Okay, okay, I'll think about it." Jennifer shook her head laughing. "And I'll report back."

Susan had been quiet all this time. With the softest of soft quilts still wrapped around her, she had curled up on Grama's sofa, listening vaguely but from far away. When she sensed a pause in the conversation she asked hesitantly, "Grama, do you think I could make a quilt? I mean, could you teach me?"

"Well, sure, Suzie honey. I would be happy to show you how," responded Grama.

"What a great idea!" Jennifer jumped in impulsively. "We could both make quilts and work on them each month when we come to see you, Grama."

"I'd really like to," Susan nodded.

Grama and I looked at each other, surprised. Although the girls have been around Grama's quilts all their lives, have watched her quilt, and still sleep under the quilts that Grama made when they were little, they have never shown any interest in making one themselves. Too old-fashioned. Too many other interests. Too time-consuming.

There is an expression that says, "When the student is ready, the teacher will appear." Ironically, in this case, the teacher had been ready for a long time and now the students decided to appear.

"Well, I'm game if you are." I shrugged at Grama and then added to the girls in my most hands-on-hips tone, "Okay, but do you realize how much work is involved, and how much time it will take?"

"Sure," they nodded tolerantly. Mothers are such a bore, but it's a job somebody's got to do.

"Are you prepared to make a commitment to do this? Seriously prepared to follow through, no matter what?" I pushed. "There's no point starting it if you're not going to finish."

They thought for a minute.

"Yes, Mom," they nodded again confidently. "We really want to do this."

"Wait a minute," Grama directed. "Let's make sure we understand what we're talking about. Just what is a commitment?"

"It's a promise to do something," Susan answered.

"It's also what each side undertakes in an agreement," Jennifer added.

"Yes. In this case, it's part of an agreement. You

agree to do something, and Grama agrees to do something. What's going to make it stick?" I asked.

"Everybody understanding the agreement and what is expected," Susan volunteered.

"Good. That is exactly right. So what are the expectations?" I prompted.

"Well, I guess we expect Grama to teach us to make a quilt, and Grama expects us to learn," Jennifer replied.

"That might also mean she will give you some advice along the way, which we know you guys are never good at taking, right?" I asked. "So, can we expect you to listen and follow instructions?"

"Yes, Mom," they chorused wearily.

"By the way, what happens if you don't live up to this commitment?"

"We would disappoint Grama," Susan said quickly.

"Yes. And who else?"

"You," Jennifer answered this time.

"And who else, more importantly?" I prodded.

They knew this was coming. All mothers do this. I think it's something they put in the orange juice given to new mothers at the hospital.

"We would disappoint ourselves," Jennifer answered wearily again. Susan nodded.

"Why?"

"Because in the future, no one would believe in our promises," Susan answered.

I nodded. "You would lose their trust."

Grama continued, "And so it is with any commitment you make in life. Your actions should never cause people to lose their trust in you. Commitment is one of the most important foundations of your character, and it's the basis of all your relationships, because it creates that trust."

"So, there is your first lesson on success, Jennifer. And you too, Susan," Grama pointed out. "You know girls, an old lady like me has a lot of time to think about life and what seems to create happiness for people."

"How do you mean, Grama?" Susan asked.

"Back on the farm when all the women would gather to quilt, sometimes we'd play the radio and listen to news from around the world. Like you, Jennifer, we young women wanted to broaden our horizons by experiencing the romance and glamour of travel, but the old women laughed at us and said they knew everything they needed to know from sitting in their front parlor quilting. In the end, I grew to understand what they meant. I've done some of my best thinking while quilting and realized that every step in making a quilt is a metaphor for what we need to do in life. I've come up with what I call the Twelve Golden Threads. Each one represents an important quality of your character. How you weave those threads through all your experiences and decisions will ultimately determine the meaning and success of your life."

"Why threads, Grama?" Jennifer asked. "I mean, I know you're a quilter and everything but . . ." Her question trailed off.

"I call them threads because, like a never-ending spool of thread, you must continue to unwind them throughout your entire life. It isn't something you just do once and are done with. Your values are like threads woven back and forth to create a whole piece of cloth, a whole life. The stronger the threads, the stronger the fabric, and, the stronger the fabric, the better the quilt will be. Similarly with life, the stronger your character, the more successful and happy you will be."

"I like that idea, Grama. 'Golden threads for success.' One of them must be commitment, like we just talked about, right? What are the others?" Susan asked.

Grama nodded yes. "The first golden thread is Make a Commitment. If we continue to use a quilt as our example, I think the other golden threads will make more sense if we talk about them as we come to the appropriate point in the work we do on your quilt. I promise to let you know when we come across the others. For now, remember that the first golden thread is Make a Commitment," Grama instructed.

"Commitment is fueled by your desire. The more you want something, the more committed you will be to achieving it," I repeated. "Now, if you are prepared to make a commitment, and want to start a quilt, then the first thing you need to do is decide when you want to finish it," I said.

They looked at me, surprised.

"We haven't even started yet! How can we know when we will be finished?" Jennifer demanded.

"I didn't say *know* when you'll finish, but when you *want* to finish. Think of the quilt as a goal. You've set goals before, and you know the acronym G–O–A–L–S stands for Goal Oriented Action Leads to Success," I reminded them.

"Could Set a Goal be another golden thread, Grama?" Susan anticipated.

Grama nodded, "Yes. Very good. You see, goals are like seams, like the seams in a garment, such as your jacket. They hold the whole design together. Seams give shape to the garment, and so goals give shape and direction to your life. Having direction gives you initiative."

I continued, "Remember, the process for setting a goal is to set a S–M–A–R–T goal. Make it:

Specific	So you know clearly what you are going for
Measurable	So you'll know when you have reached the goal

Achievable	So it's not an impossible day dream
Relevant	So it's important to you
Time-framed	So it's set within a finite dead line

"Without setting a deadline you are working toward a fuzzy 'someday,' and vague 'somedays' never happen. By giving yourself a doable deadline, you keep yourself motivated and focused."

"How about by Christmas?" Jennifer suggested eagerly.

"No way," Susan challenged. "Don't forget we need Grama to show us how, and I have school and studying. I have to get good grades this year or I won't get into a good college. How about by the time I graduate college?" she counteroffered.

I shook my head. Susan is an honor student but she still worries about her grades. "Oh, Suzie, that's too long," I objected. "Give yourself enough time to get the work done, but not so much that you lose your enthusiasm and start to procrastinate. Come on, challenge yourself. How about one year? By this time next year?"

"But we, I couldn't do that," whined Susan. "It takes Grama a year to make a quilt, and she's an expert. I don't know anything yet." The insecurities of her youth were showing against the surety of Grama's long experience.

"But I'm old!" Grama laughed. "There are always balances in life. See these gnarly old fingers. You young girls can do everything a lot faster than me. It's not difficult, you'll see." She smiled reassuringly. "Don't be afraid of the size of the finished quilt, or goal. Remember, the only way to eat an elephant is one bite at a time! We'll break the whole job down into little bites that will make it easier, and the time will go by fast."

"I'm still not sure I can eat an elephant in one year—even if it is one bite at a time," Susan exclaimed playfully.

"Now, Susan," Grama chided gently, "Potential obstacles to finishing a project should never discourage you from starting it in the first place. Any old fool can make a quilt if you just learn a few simple tricks. Just like life, all quilting takes is good habits. One year seems fine to me. Besides, I want to make sure I'm still around to see them finished."

"Oh, Grama, you're going to live forever," Susan asserted confidently. "Do you really think we could make quilts in a year?" Susan asked in disbelief.

Grama nodded yes.

"Okay. One year," Jennifer agreed, satisfied.

"Okay. One year," said Susan, not so convinced.

To seal the pact I summarized by saying, "So we have a commitment that each of you will complete a quilt by this time next year, by working on it step by step each month as we visit Grama."

We all nodded.

Grama mused, "Girls, designing your quilt is an excellent metaphor for designing your life. In both cases each of you is creating something that will be a piece of your future. Setting a goal is looking ahead to the future. So an important first exercise is to picture in your mind's eye exactly what you want the goal, the quilt, or even the future to look like. See it in as much detail as possible. Make it big and in full-color."

"Professional golfers do that, don't they?" Susan said. "They practice their golf swing in their head before they go out and play. I've heard they can actually improve their swing by first going through the motions mentally."

Grama smiled as she continued, "That's right. And you can also add to the picture how great you'll feel when you have accomplished it. The more joy and enthusiasm you can feel in imagining it, the easier the work will be, and the more motivated you will be to realize the goal."

"How do we start, Grama?" they asked.

"We start," she replied, "by going down to Ivy's restaurant and having some lunch. She has pumpkin pie today, and I don't want to miss it. After that, I'll give you some of my quilt books and magazines. You can take them home and decide what pattern you want to make and what colors you like. Both of you will have lots of fun decisions to make as you design your quilts.

"The next time you visit, we'll split the work into bite-sized pieces and set up your action plan to get the work done," Grama concluded as we headed off to lunch.

On the way home, Jennifer and Susan looked through Grama's quilt magazines. I told them how happy I was that they had decided to make quilts. It's a special experience to share with Grama, and Grama is a terrific role model for them.

"Find someone who is already expert and successful at what you want to do and let them be a role model for you. Learn from them, copy what they do, and take to heart the lessons they have to tell. You can't go wrong that way.

"Role models," I explained, "help us by giving us examples of how to achieve a goal and also examples of what it sometimes costs to do so."

"What do you mean?" Susan asked.

"There is always a price to pay," I warned, "either emotionally, in time and energy, or even in giving up something else that is less important to us. In fact, even negative role models can show us what we should not be doing or what it could cost if we *don't* realize our goals."

"That sounds like another one of Grama's golden threads to me," Jennifer teased.

"Hmmm. Not quite. I think you'll find that following the golden threads is a process that builds your character and results in what we would call right behavior. Role models simply smooth the road ahead by acting as examples. You could think of them as the basting threads that you use in sewing as a guideline for the finished stitches," I said, drawing a fabric analogy for her.

Jennifer continued, "So, for example, I should find out who is the most successful broker at my bank and follow what he or she does?"

"Yes, that's the idea," I confirmed.

"Mom?" It was Susan, puzzled. "Should you go and ask people for their advice, like 'How did you become successful?'"

"That is one way, sure. Often in business or in the trades, an executive or a more experienced lead hand will take on a junior, or apprentice, like Grama is doing with you, and show them the ropes. It's called mentoring. But a role model could be anyone. Even someone you don't know. They don't have to know you are copying them," I answered.

Jennifer asked, "What's the difference between a role model and a heroine?"

"There is a subtle difference," I explained. "A heroine is someone you admire for their qualities of character, and want to be like. As the word role implies, a role model is someone you want to act like. You may not even care for them as people. For example, you might dislike a particular athlete because she's bad-tempered and arrogant, but you could follow her successful role or formula of practicing every day, eating the right foods, and so on. Does that make sense?"

They both nodded.

"But a role model could be a heroine as well," Jennifer suggested.

"Yes," I agreed.

"Could role models be historical characters or famous people?" Susan asked. "One of my teachers said that Mother Teresa is a great teacher. So since I want to teach, studying Mother Teresa would help me become a better teacher?"

"That's it," I encouraged. "Once you get to know and understand the role model, whenever you are in a situation you can ask yourself, How would so-and-so handle this? It's a great way to make easier decisions. Simply create a mental council of advisors, comprised of people whose opinions you respect, and ask for their guidance and advice. You see, we often choose our role models in life because they represent our own inner ideal self."

"Could I put Grama on my council?" Susan asked.

"You sure could. She is someone I would always want to have on my team," I agreed. "I want to suggest one precaution however. Be sure that your role model's version of success and how to achieve it is the same as yours. So again, you will want to be clear on what success means to you." I directed this to Jennifer.

"Making money," she replied, confidently and stubbornly.

"At any cost? Even if it means stealing or lying, for example? If the role model you chose made crooked deals, would you follow their lead?" I asked.

"No, of course not!"

"Good. But what if they worked twenty hours a day to get success?"

"I'm prepared to work that hard if need be."

"I'm sure you are. But what if that meant you never had time to date, fall in love, and have a family? Or, if you married and your work put so much stress on the relationship that you ended up divorced? Would that be success to you, even if you made lots of money?"

"No. But that wouldn't happen to me."

"Sweetie, no one ever plans to have disasters happen. But you can prevent problems or at least lessen their impact if you are prepared for the possible outcome of your choices, the hidden costs, and if you plan accordingly. As we said, along with knowing what success is, and why you want it, you need to realize what it will cost you and what it will cost if you don't achieve it. That's why we study the examples of role models, so that we can make wiser choices."

I paused to let Jennifer think. Her lips were

pressed together in a thin line of consternation. I've been a reasonably well-respected professional psychologist for fifteen years, ever since Susan went to preschool. Although my degree is in industrial psychology and I worked for several years at a large corporation, I retired temporarily to have children. When I returned to full-time work, my focus had shifted and I decided to go into private counseling practice. As a result, at home I always walk a thin line between being "Mom" and being "the shrink." Sometimes I push too hard and Jennifer, the family barometer, lets me know it. They don't always want to hear what Dr. Mom has to say. Sometimes I think they would have preferred Betty Crocker.

"If you do one thing, the cost may be that you can't do something else. If you become a doctor, you probably don't also get to become a lawyer. Obviously you can't do everything. Okay, so what?" Jennifer argued petulantly.

"But you can choose to be happy," I answered, "by ensuring that all the decisions you make about your life are ones that give you satisfaction. And that may have nothing to do with money. What I'm saying, honey, is success can mean different things to different people, at different times. Surprisingly enough, not everyone wants to be a millionaire. There are many ways to be successful and many ways to achieve success. For example, you would probably agree that

Gandhi was an extremely successful person, but he didn't own a thing. He had a tremendous impact on his people. That was important to him. He was successful at what he tried to do for them, but even he didn't accomplish everything he wanted to."

"So, if success is different all the time and if it isn't measured by stuff, or what you earn, or even by what you accomplish, then what is success?" Now Jennifer was perplexed, struggling for a concrete answer. She was growing frustrated. By nature, Jennifer is gregarious, optimistic, and enthusiastic. She's more likely to respond emotionally than to think things through logically. She wants to take action, sometimes like a shotgun—scattered and explosive. It bothers her when she doesn't easily understand things.

"Well, there is one definition of success that may make it easier for you," I explained. "Success can be viewed as simply the continued forward movement toward a goal, whatever that goal may be. In other words, it's the *process*, not the product," I told her.

She thought for a long minute, then said, "I see. And a successful person, then, is someone who constantly works toward their goals. They would be successful, even if they don't actually reach their goal," she observed.

"Right. And when they do reach one goal, they

set another. Success in this definition is not the thing itself, it's staying on the path toward the goal. If you make that your definition of success you make your life a lot happier, because you can be successful all of the time, not just at the end."

The girls were looking at me with puzzled expressions so I continued with an example. "I think the best adventures are in the traveling. If the trip to your destination lasts ten days, you only arrive once, on the tenth day. But you travel for nine days to get there. I would rather be happy and feel successful for nine days than for just one. And, as you pointed out, I can feel successful even if I never arrive," I explained.

"I like that idea." The frown finally left Jennifer's face. "And I could take side trips along the way, too, I guess." I smiled at that. Yes, Jennifer is easily distracted.

"Of course. It's during the traveling that all the interesting things happen and all the opportunities to learn present themselves. Just like your quilt projects. It will be wonderful to have them completed, but I suspect that what happens along the way as you work on them will be the thought-provoking events. And your enjoyment of the finished quilt will be heightened by the memories of your experience in creating it."

"So it all comes back to how important it is to

have goals—Grama's second golden thread," Susan reflected.

"Okay. I'm definitely going to think about this goal-setting and success stuff," Jennifer relented. "Will you help me?"

"Of course I will. How about you, Susan?" I asked.

"Oh, well, of course goal-setting is important but all that success stuff is for Jennifer. She's the one with ambition. I just want to teach," she replied with a shrug. She had participated in the discussions but apparently only by proxy for her sister's benefit.

"But don't you want to be a successful teacher?" Jennifer rebuked her.

"It's not the same thing," she huffed.

"So you think the things Grama is saying don't apply to you and the decisions you're making in life just because you already have a career picked out." I left the implied question hanging.

Susan looked at me thoughtfully for several moments. "Hmm," she said finally, quietly, with realization.

I raised my eyebrows and nodded a confirming "Hmm." For all her book smarts sometimes the obvious goes whizzing by her.

"So, just as you design your quilt, goals are how both of you design your life. Once you know what you want, why you want it, and what the cost is, then the first exercise is to imagine it in your mind's eye," I recapped Grama's formula. "And the second exercise is to find and follow a role model."

"A role model like Grama," Susan suggested.

"Yes. Now about those quilts, girls, let's be clear. If this quilt thing is just a whim-for-today, please think carefully and decide now. Grama will understand if you want to cancel the quilt project," I prodded, but they were already flipping through the quilt magazines, oo-oohing and aahing over a color scheme, a splashy design, and mostly criticizing each other's choices as "stoo-oo-pid," as sisters will.

As we drove home, I mused to myself about the curious and surprising turns in life one day can provide.

So we were to be plunged into a year of quilting. The commitment was made, even though no one yet knew what "it" would look like exactly, or what actions "it" would take to achieve. We had a time frame too. A one-year goal. They were starting to visualize the final outcome and Grama would be their role model.

As we pulled into our driveway I was content and peaceful. This was a good beginning, I thought. The girls were excited. I felt happy and proud of my young women. There would be lots to learn in the upcoming year.

*G*OLDEN *T*HREAD #1

Make a Commitment

*G*OLDEN *T*HREAD #2

Set a Goal

NOVEMBER
First Steps

We were late starting out this morning. Grama had called with a request.

"If Robbie's not wearing that red shirt with the little purple sailboats on it anymore, I can cut it up and use it on my new quilt. Have the girls picked out their patterns? Good. See you soon. Drive carefully. We had a little slippery snow here last night."

Grama never likes to see anything go to waste, wants to use up everything, and has a steel-trap memory. Her old-fashioned frugality born in the necessities of her youth, is newly refound in country-wide recycling programs born from environmental necessity. Old is new again.

So the shirt had to be found. I figure when you get to be eighty-five, people shouldn't disappoint you.

Robbie hadn't worn that particular shirt in years. It had been Jack's. When he died, Robbie wore it every day for a month. He was thirteen at the time. Even the boys at school, usually so boisterous and insensitive, backed off from teasing him about the garish shirt. I didn't have the heart to stop him. Truth is, I wished I could have done the same thing myself, still held Jack around me. I only made Robbie wash the shirt, which he did, quietly, by himself, by hand. I never knew what it was but sensed there was a memory in it, of a shared time, a father-son time, that he needed to keep alive. How instinctively we hold on to symbols.

Looking back now, I see I was lucky because keeping the household and three children going made it easier on me. Counseling others, I found myself saying the things to them that I needed to hear myself. The unbearable pain faded to a dull ache. Like a train pulling away from a station, it receded as it stayed in the past and slowly moved further and further away into distant memory. After a while, the shirt was seldom worn, then not at all, and finally it was released to the scrap material basket.

Now, happily, it was wanted again. Grama's quilts are always a wonderful montage of old and new, connections crisscrossing time. She collects, sorts, debates, chooses, and brings swatches of colorful past into the present, materially and metaphorically. Women connect viscerally to metaphors, not only in words, but in their lives. Our simple everyday acts take on a deeply symbolic and personal meaning. Besides, it's fun to find the memories in Grama's quilts.

Nearing eighty-five, Grama's "now" is more heavily weighted with the past than with the future, except for the times like these when she is passing on her knowledge to our girls. They will be the future.

Since Grama never learned to drive, we like to take her out to special places whenever possible. This was our Thanksgiving meal. We had a great deal to be thankful for. As I watched Grama and the girls I realized how much I enjoy my "middle age." I'm comfortable in the middle, between Grama's wisdom and tranquillity, and my children's innocence and enthusiasm.

"This is what I want to make, Grama." Jennifer was all smiles as she opened the book to her design, a riotous rainbow of colors. We had arrived in time for a late lunch and were all sitting around a festively decorated table at a local restaurant.

Jennifer pushed the dishes aside to make room for her magazine. "Isn't it gorgeous? It's so bright and modern."

True to her nature, she had picked a spectacular design without worrying about the details of how she would complete it. Her enthusiasm sometimes gives her a rash fearlessness in the face of challenge.

"Hmmm," Grama possibly agreed, casting her experienced eye over the page. "Well, that will certainly be a challenge for you."

"Pretty ambitious," I nodded, thinking, maybe too much so. Would I ever stop seeing her as the little girl constantly reaching for things beyond her grasp? The instinct is to overprotect, but didn't we always teach them to stretch themselves?

"If she doesn't go *blind* working on it," chided Susan. "Look at all the little tiny pieces. It's so busy-looking."

"That makes it *interesting*. At least mine won't be boring," Jennifer taunted back. "Like *yours*," she added under her breath.

"You'll never *finish* yours. You know you never finish anything you start," smirked Susan.

"No one will ever bother to *look* at yours," Jennifer retorted snootily.

This is a family that talks in italics. *A lot.*

"Let's see your design, Susan," Grama interrupted somewhat impatiently.

Susan had chosen a simple traditional pattern of "Churn and Dash" with "Flying Geese" around the border, done in muted calico prints. It would be a safe and tentative beginning. Having made a commitment, Susan picked something that she figured she could finish. Unlike her sister, Susan is shy, cautious, and introspective, and her concern would always be doing it right or not at all. How did I manage to produce two such different daughters? Here I was in the middle again. I could see myself in both of them.

"At least mine won't keep me awake at night. Or glow in the dark and give me nightmares." Susan started again at Jennifer.

"And this has been going on for a month now," I sighed wearily to Grama. I only have one older brother and I used to wonder what having a sister was like. I've learned a lot about sisters from my daughters. I never envy their squabbles, but on the good days their camaraderie makes me wish I had a sister. Maybe that's why I've grown closer to Grama over the years. At some point as people grow older, time seems to stop. Grama is standing still and I'm catching up to her as I age. If she waits for me, someday perhaps we will be old sisters together. The fact of our chronological difference will be lost in the synchronous rhythm of our rocking-chair wisdom.

Grama just smiled, ignored the banter, and said, "Well, that's good. You both chose something different. Each choice complements your different personalities. Just as in a career, Susan, you want to be a teacher, and you, Jennifer, want to be in business. First of all, it's important that your choices in life are congruent with your personality and your values. When your actions are in tune with your inner self and your beliefs, you have contentment, or inner harmony. Us old folks call it, 'To thine own Self, be true.'"

"In psychological terms," I continued, "behaving in a way that is incongruent with what you believe to be correct is one of the fastest roads to unhappiness and inner turmoil. Often people are not consciously aware that they are causing themselves such grief, or they won't admit that they are. You achieve peace of mind only with congruency between your actions and your beliefs. That's why money can't buy happiness, Jen, if the money came from incongruent actions."

Grama nodded and smiled. "And, of course, the other side of congruency is acceptance of others. Jennifer, your design is bold, ambitious, and beautiful. Susan, yours is gentle, and peaceful, and beautiful. You are both different young women. Let each other be different. Value and support the contrast and be happy that you are not carbon copies of each other. Life is more interesting because people have different thoughts and ideas, and 'designs.' Know what is right for you, and accept what may be right for someone else—and support their being congruent to themselves."

I jumped in here, "And like us middle-aged folks say, 'beauty is in the eye of the beholder.' What is beautiful? Susan, you say A, and Jennifer, you say B. You are both right. The truth is, reality is how you choose to see life." I picked up a waterglass and tapped it. "You know the expression: Is the glass half-empty or half-full? It all depends on your perspective."

"Isn't that what you've always said about 'walk a mile in someone else's shoes?'" Susan asked. "See things from their point of view, a different point of view?"

"Yes," I laughed. "I didn't realize I taught you so many clichés."

"You sure did," Jennifer teased. "Don't count your chickens before they hatch."

"Never put off until tomorrow what can be done today," Susan chimed in.

"Don't cry over spilt milk," Jennifer added.

"Okay, okay. It comes with the territory," I said in my defense. "But in any case," I continued, bringing them back to the point, "the process of growth and maturity does require us to see things differently. If I want reality or life to change, then first I must change. I must be prepared to alter how I view life. Failure to recognize when it's time to let go of an idea, attitude, or behavior, is fatal to success, for an individual, a company, or even a society. In a world where change comes to us at an ever-increasing rate, the ability to shift thinking is crucial. Change is another word for time. Time allows us to watch the waterglass and see whether it is filling or emptying. That knowledge allows us to adapt. If you make it an attitude habit to be open to change you will always feel confident in your ability to cope, and that helps eliminate fear of the future and the uncertainties we all face."

Grama nodded. "If you are both right in your interpretation of a beautiful quilt, and therefore neither of you is wrong, can you not then support each other's viewpoint without it diminishing or threatening your own? Yes? Good, then take off the boxing gloves, come out and shake hands. We have lots of work to do. Okay? Okay."

"Grama is right," Susan acquiesced. "And like Mom said, your goal looks different than mine, but it's the path we take that matters."

"Okay. And right now we are both on the same path, with Grama as our guide. It doesn't matter what the destination is, it's the traveling that counts, right, Mom? So how do we start this journey in quiltland, Grama?" Jennifer inquired.

"That is where your plan for action comes in," Grama continued. "We already discussed how important it is that your actions are congruent with your values. Now it is time to discuss the plan itself.

"Remember, the first golden thread is Make a Commitment and the second is Set a Goal. The third golden thread for success is Plan Your Work and Work Your Plan. Write the plan down. In the same way that you use a paper dress pattern, your plan is your 'paper pattern' for success. I would never set out to make a quilt without designing it on paper first. In fact, I find that the process of writing down the plan reinforces my commitment and keeps me focused on the steps I have to take to reach my goal. That's S–T–E–P–S, an easy-to-remember acronym. It stands for Simple, Time-framed, Efficient, Prioritized, and Start now.

"The 'S' stands for *simple*. Keep your plan as simple as possible. Strip it down until you are left with the most important action items. Then, break down the project into smaller tasks or actions that are easy to handle.

"The 'T' stands for *time-framed*. Set a date for each mini task to be completed.

"The 'E' stands for *efficient*. That means you consider all the possible courses of action and determine which one will take you from start to finish in the most direct way, in the least time.

"The 'P' stands for *prioritized*, which means you order each item according to its importance and urgency, in the sequence it needs to be performed. Don't put the cart before the horse. In other words, do first things first." Grama paused as she cleaned her glasses.

"Steps," Susan repeated. "That's easy to remember. Simple, time-framed, efficient, and prioritized."

The girls nodded as I continued, "You see, planning should be the easiest part of the process. It is just thinking through logically from start to finish, identifying all the necessary actions. The execution of the plan should be the hard part. Too often, though, people get stuck in the planning process itself."

"I know what you mean, Mom. I have friends who are always talking about their plans to do something, but never get anything done," Susan agreed. "My friend Kendra has been planning to sew herself a prom dress but she never does anything about it. Every time I ask her about it she has some excuse. When she's got some money, she goes to the movies. If she has a free weekend, she goes skiing. She has lots of plans and good intentions but something always seems to come up."

"Sounds like Emma's dilemma," I commented.

"What's that?" she asked.

"A few years ago I had a client named Emma who used to say she was determined to get out of debt but every time she was faced with making a financial decision, she too went for the short-term satisfaction. She wanted a better job but she wasn't prepared to work evenings or weekends to obtain one. In fact, she ended up spending money instead of taking the opportunity to earn some. It's a common dilemma. It comes from confusion about what your true priorities are. In spite of what people say, it's what people do that really identifies their underlying values and desires. If you say you want financial security but go skiing every weekend, you are just fooling yourself. You have to either bring your actions in line with your avowed goal, or, admit to yourself that you really want to put pleasure first and security second in your list of priorities. In fact, that's sort of a foolproof way to make the right decision every time you make a decision. Be clear about your true priorities in life. If you are clear about your intention, then planning the steps to get you there is easy."

"Last year at school," Jennifer recounted, "a girl in my class and I hung out together. She told me she had this terrific study plan on her computer. At first I was impressed. Every week she showed me a new printout of her schedule and how much time she had left to finish her term papers. Then I noticed she kept planning and replanning and rescheduling the same work, the same essays and studies, but nothing happened.

"As the deadlines approached, she started coming in every day with a new plan, still convinced she could get everything done. If she had spent some of the time she wasted in planning on doing real work, she might have achieved something. After a while I couldn't stand being around her!"

"That is a typical example, Jen, of someone being part-smart," I assured her. "Try not to let that negative example dissuade you though. The important thing is, once you have a workable plan, do the work! It doesn't have to be perfect before you get into gear. A plan is not a substitute for work. It's only there to keep you on track and focused. That's why it's called a plan for action, not a plan for plans. Do you know which is the most important of the S–T–E–P–S?"

"Which one?" Susan dutifully asked.

"The last one. The final 'S' stands for *start now*. You have to act on the plan. Nothing gets done until you start. A plan without action is just an idle dream. Like your friend, Jen—she never settled down to doing her work."

"One final point about planning: If making and keeping commitments is a value that builds your character as a person to be trusted, what quality do you think following through on a plan shows about you?" Grama asked.

"That you are hard-working," Jennifer tried.

"Yes, and what makes you hard-working?" Grama prompted.

"Umm, persistence," Susan guessed.

"Sort of. What makes you persistent?"

"Discipline?"

"Right. Self-discipline." Grama nodded, satisfied. "Do you think that might be a quality employers out there in the working world value in employees?" I suggested.

"Sure. Because they would know you are organized and finish your work without them having to check up on you all the time," Susan answered.

"So, do you think people can succeed without self-discipline?"

"No way," they affirmed.

"And that's why Plan Your Work and Work Your Plan is the numbe-three golden thread," Grama confirmed.

We had returned to Grama's apartment and for the rest of the peaceful afternoon, Grama taught Jennifer and Susan how to create cardboard templates, which are used to cut each individual piece of fabric for their designs. She then showed them how to calculate the total areas and to convert that to fabric yardage for purchase. They found it easier than they expected. All it took was some simple math and grade school geometry.

By the time we left, Jennifer and Susan had their plan for action for the upcoming year written out month by month. They had all their S—T—E—P—S. Their plan was simple, time-framed, efficient, prioritized, and they had started.

They knew exactly how much of each color fabric they needed for the quilt top and the backing. They had prepared a budget. We had agreed on a schedule to shop for material. They were prepared with second choices and alternative ideas in case they could not find what they wanted or could afford. They had limited funds: most of Susan's money from a part-time job at a grocery store after school went into saving for college tuition; and Jennifer's entry-level salary was used to buy a new "professional" wardrobe. I was tempted to help them out but thought that they would value their quilts more if it came from the sweat of their own brows so to speak, as well as their own hands.

We were ready to start.

Their quilt projects had been broken down into smaller tasks that were doable in the month between visits to Grama. First, they would prewash and iron all the fabric and arrive next month ready to start cutting all the quilt pieces. In the following months, they would sew the quilt top together, add the batting and backing materials, and baste it all together. Once these pieces were sewn together, they would do all the hand quilting and add the final binding. And lastly, they'd sign and date the finished quilts, and celebrate the achievement. There would be lots to do.

"Plan your work and work your plan," Jack used to say as he taught all our children how to do their homework assignments. It never dawned on me that he had learned to do the same thing at his mother's knee, Grama's knee. In those days she would never have talked to a son about quilting the way she does now with Jennifer and Susan, but the values and the seeds of her wisdom were obviously already growing years ago. Somehow she had managed to translate her experience and values into lessons that Jack and his brothers had understood and assimilated. He had become a supportive, "feminist" husband and father before it was recognized or popular. Clearly women's wisdom and values can be communicated to men, in meaningful ways without beating them over the head.

Plan your work and work your plan. Here were our girls doing exactly that. Jack would have been proud.

Grama had spun three of her golden threads. We had a commitment, a goal, and now a plan for action. So far, things were working out just fine.

Golden Thread #3

Plan Your Work and Work Your Plan

DECEMBER
Measure Twice, Cut Once

Christmas is always a wonderful and hectic time of the year around our house. So much coming and going. So many ups and downs. Some friction, lots of hugs. Snapshot memories linger for a while, then float like leaves in the autumn, falling to the forest floor, forming a rich soil that will nourish new growth in the spring.

I teased Robbie that all he brought me for Christmas was his laundry. The girls hung his dirty sweatsocks on the mantel for stockings. He stole their pantyhose and garlanded the tree with them. On Christmas Eve, I had the last say. In each of their stockings I placed a mini box of laundry detergent with a photocopy of the washing machine instructions. Silly family humor.

Someone says, "I miss Dad," and we are all quiet for a while.

The doorbell rings and neighbors bluster in for holiday cookies and eggnog, stamping their feet, shaking snow and filling the house with loud cheery greetings. The girls are particularly pleased with the "oohs" and "aahs" over their carefully decorated tree. Somehow I can't remember ever seeing an ugly Christmas tree.

"You know I always try to give you girls different things for Christmas," Grama explained as she handed them packages on Christmas morning, "but this year it seems appropriate that you both have the same thing."

They quickly opened the presents.

"Grama, this is terrific. My own sewing kit." Susan enthused. "Now we don't have to borrow Mom's stuff."

"Borrow and lose," Jennifer corrected. "This is great. Look, Mom, everything we could ever need to sew with. Thanks, Grama!" She hugged Grama affectionately.

Grama had carefully assembled dressmakers' tape measures, rulers, pins and pincushions with an elastic band to wear around the wrist, regular needles and quilting needles, called betweens. She included a rotary cutter with extra blades and a cutting board, a pair of superior quality fabric shears along with a cheap pair of scissors for cutting paper, a seam-ripper and small thread snips on a cord to wear around the neck to keep them handy. She had thought of everything.

The presents propelled Jennifer and Susan right into their quilting work. They were eager to try out their new gifts, so we hurried dressing and breakfast and then assembled around the diningroom table. Jennifer and Susan brought their shopping bags with fabric. Robbie waved off their invitation to join us and plugged his headphones into the CD player. Sometimes a house full of women is too overwhelming even for him. Wearing headphones and sitting with his clean white socks on the coffee table, he looked so much like Jack did as a young college man, it made tears come to my eyes. Grama saw me watching Robbie and smiled. Patting my hand reassuringly, she said, "He's his mother's boy too, you know."

"Today we do some real work," Grama began cheerfully, taking her place at the head of the table. "You know, someone once said that a quilt is a self-portrait of the person who made it. So be sure to autograph your work with excellence. Golden thread number four is Always Do Quality Work. Maybe that's an old fuddy-duddy idea. But, I want to see you do your best. Okay?"

"It's not so old-fashioned, Grama," I replied. "These days in the business world people are returning to the traditional values of quality and service.

People are tired of shoddy goods and being treated poorly by supposed customer service people. Businesses are finally waking up to customers who are saying, 'I'll take my money elsewhere.' That hits them in the pocketbook."

"Too bad they are being forced into it," Grama rued. "I wish they were doing right just because it is right. Anyway, I guess we can't change that." Grama shrugged and carried on. "Now, let me see the fabrics you chose for your quilts," she directed.

She inspected each one and finally pronounced, "You made excellent choices. These are good quality fabrics that will last. Did your mom help you pick them out? No? Then you instinctively did the right thing.

"Quilting is an old tradition. It's a throwback to the times of pride in craftsmanship and handwork. You could buy a cheap factory-made quilt, but you decided to invest the time to make this quilt yourself. You want to do it well and to make sure that the work lasts. Strive for quality. When excellence is what you put in your work, quality is the result. Quality work lasts.

"You can always coast through life by meeting minimum standards of performance, but quality work always exceeds minimum expectations," Grama concluded.

"How do you do that?" Susan asked.

"I've found that there are some simple rules to

follow that produce quality craftsmanship in whatever you do. Rule one is start with the best possible materials. You've all heard 'you can't make a silk purse out of a sow's ear.' Although personally, I don't know why anyone would try! Seriously, top-grade fabric, not cheap stuff that will fall apart, leads to a superior finished product."

"Makes sense," Jennifer nodded. "What's the second rule, Grama?"

"Rule two is use the best tools for the job. Good tools make a job easier, more exact, more efficient. Whether it's painting a house or painting a watercolor masterpiece, there is a right brush for the job. That's why I gave you sewing supplies for Christmas—I wanted to make sure you have the best tools to work with on your quilts."

"Guess we might have known there was an ulterior motive!" Susan laughed, and then asked, "Is there a third rule?"

"Of course! Rule three is hone your skills. In other words, know what you are doing. Whether you're sewing, handling customers, teaching mathematics, or reading financial reports, practice all the time to improve your skills."

"Practice makes perfect," Jennifer quoted.

"No. Perfect practice makes perfect," Grama promptly corrected. "If you keep doing the wrong things over and over all you improve is how to do things wrong. Do the right things over and over.

That's how you make skillful work into a success habit."

"Makes sense. Rule four?" Jennifer prompted.

"Rule four is work carefully. Simply that. No mystery to it. Work carefully. Think and pay attention to details. In quilting, there is a saying: 'measure twice, cut once.' It means you measure and then remeasure before you cut the material. Being careful prevents wasteful errors.

"And what would rule five be?" Grama asked mischievously.

"Reread rules one, two, three, and four," we chorused.

"By Jove, I think they've got it!" Grama laughed happily. "Those rules are my 'work-to-rule' attitude habit."

Grama then showed Jennifer and Susan how to cut the fabric pieces using a rotary cutter. To explain it simply, a rotary cutter looks just like a pizza cutting wheel, only it's very, very sharp for cutting through layers of sometimes thick material. A reasonably new invention, it decreased fabric cutting time from hours, to minutes. For quilters, who are often cutting hundreds of pieces of fabric, it is truly the "greatest thing since sliced pizza."

The girls worked at opposite ends of the dining room table as Grama talked. Jennifer, who had many more intricate pieces to cut, was looking for a short-cut and had decided to fold over her fabric several times so that she could cut a dozen pieces at once. Grama let her continue with this method for a few minutes, then stopped her and inspected the quality of her work. As Grama suspected, the multiple layers allowed for more slipping of the material and many pieces turned out not to be the required dimensions of the templates.

"Okay, let's talk here for a minute." Grama interrupted the work. "Jennifer, why did you decide to fold the material the way you did?"

"To cut more pieces at once. To be more efficient like you said we should be," she defended.

"That is what I thought and I commend you. Willingness to work efficiently is an excellent attitude to have. However, we need to be clear on what efficiency is. Most people think efficiency simply means doing the work as fast as possible. We say machines are more efficient and they work quickly, so we have come to think the terms are synonymous."

"Yeah, but unfortunately, Grama, many employers also operate with that in mind and pressure employees to function that way too," Jennifer pointed out. "That's the way it is in business today."

"Well, that's not right!" Grama replied indignantly. "In order to do quality work and to be efficient as well, you have to strike a balance between accuracy and time. As you found out, Jen, the more you cut at once, the faster you were but the less accurate each piece became. You will have to go back and correct those pieces. So the saved time becomes wasted time. Sometimes going slower is faster in the long run."

Jennifer grimaced at the prospect.

"You see, dear, there is no absolute efficiency; it is always relative to an objective. There are times," Grama continued, "when exact accuracy is not as important. That is a judgment you have to make about each situation, taking your objective into account. Sometimes it's okay to approximate and then accuracy may not be terribly critical. But in this case, accuracy is important. If you have even a small mistake in each piece of fabric, the error will accumulate across the quilt as you sew, and you will never make the final pieces fit together properly."

"So efficiency is always the balance of accuracy against time," Jennifer repeated unhappily as she contemplated the small pile of pieces she had cut.

I tried to console her. Putting my arm around her shoulder I said, "Trust Grama. She knows. You may feel frustrated now at redoing the work, but imagine how upset you would be if you'd sewn it all together and then found out it didn't fit."

Jennifer sighed. She wasn't happy about it but quickly resigned herself to going back and correcting all the work that she had done.

At the other end of the table, Susan had kept her head down, slowly and meticulously cutting her fabric one piece at a time. It looked like she was relieved to be out of the line of fire so to speak. Quieter than her older and outspoken sister, Susan often had the opportunity to learn from the mistakes that Jennifer the trailblazer made. I'm sure Susan felt overshadowed by her bombastic sister, but there were times when it had a distinct advantage. Sometimes older siblings leave behind expectations and a reputation in the minds of teachers and friends that the younger ones have trouble living up to. One way that Susan established her individuality was by being smarter sooner. I remember learning lessons by proxy through my older brother.

"The more you do, the less accurate the work becomes," I repeated and mused as I watched them continue their work. "You can also take it to mean that in life the more you do, if you spread yourself too thin, the less you are able to focus on, and excel at, any one thing. Another success choice you may have to make, Jen.

"Since there are still only twenty-four hours in a day, you can choose to do one thing reasonably well, or, you can do many things, perhaps poorly."

"But, Mom," Jennifer interrupted, "these days women are often involved in a lot of different things at the same time. Look at our friends and neighbors. Some of them are career woman, wife, mother, Girl Guide leader, church goer, and so on. There are so many things to do these days, and they all seem to require different parts of our personality and make demands on our time. How can you not be spread too thin? What's the answer?"

"There are two answers," Grama offered. "The first is to focus intently on one thing at a time. Do each thing with one hundred percent attention and maximize your energy and time. In simple terms, when you play, play. When you work, work.

"You are right, Jen," she continued. "There are a lot of demands of women. Unfortunately, the danger is, if we take on too many things, we may not succeed at any of them. It's important to know when to say no—to make active decisions for yourself rather than be forced by circumstances, or other people's agendas, into being reactive and out of control. Make sure you are making your own choices."

"And the second thing," I added, "is that you have to learn to prioritize what you do and to differentiate between what is important versus what is urgent. Urgency is often impelled on us by other people's agendas. What is urgent may not in the long run be important. For example, many people have been seduced into the corporate rat race by the lure of power and money. Movies and television make it all look glamorous, exciting, and enviable. But for many women it means they have been given an added pressure to succeed in business, or professionally, along with everything else. There's an expectation that women should *want* to work outside the home. It's made a lot of mothers feel guilty that their role as stay-home mom isn't good enough or successful enough for a modern woman. I'm not saying that women shouldn't seek high-level positions. I'm just saying not everyone—male or female—has the strength or desire to achieve a top executive position. And not everyone wants to, or should be expected to want it.

"Nowadays people are reevaluating their choices. Society holds out the proverbial brass ring of 'having it all.' Many people discovered this comes at an unacceptable high cost. They now see that high-level corporate success in many cases is bought at the price of human connectedness. Even some men have realized that actively raising your children can be more satisfying than an executive job, a big income, and the gold washroom key. The work we do for a living is urgent work but inevitably, unfortunately we are all expendable and replaceable. I'd like to think that the work we do raising our families is important. It's the true legacy we pass on to future generations and the true contribution we make to society. In my counseling practice I see many lonely, stressed executives, who are outwardly successful but can't figure out why their lives feel like such a shambles to them, why they're alienated from their wives, and their children are strangers.

"Many people are now prepared to renounce that supposed higher level of worldly success for a less visible, and often unrewarded role in society, such as staying home to raise a family or pursuing the career they love even if it never makes them a fortune. Having it all is not so great as having the best," I said.

Grama concluded with, "So be aware of the choices you are making. Decide how and where you expend your lifework energy, how wide or narrow your focus is. And most important, remember that your choices will define the quality of your life and your relationships, professional and personal." She turned and nodded to Jennifer. "Something else to take into consideration as you define success for yourself and set your goals in life."

I noticed that Jennifer was being less defensive in these discussions. She seemed quieter and more willing to listen. It was interesting to watch her thinking and reexamining her opinions and options.

The fabric cutting was incomplete by the time we had to move on to preparing Christmas dinner so Grama set Jennifer and Susan the task of having their fabric cut out by next month's visit, and she showed them how to mark the back of each piece so they would know where each one fit into the overall design. However, there were a lot of social activities to keep us busy and so the quilt projects lay temporarily forgotten until after the holidays.

Eventually, Robbie flew back to college and we drove Grama back to Clareville. In the car on the way home again I decided to pursue another thought about work with the girls.

"What's the most important aspect of work itself, in the sense of your job or employment?" I asked.

"I don't know which is the most important, but like Grama said," Susan started, thinking I was calling for a review of Grama's golden thread number four on quality work. "Start with the best materials. Use the right tools. Hone your skills. Work carefully."

"That's good. That is exactly what Grama's rules were. That is how to work. I asked the wrong question. Let me try again. What is work itself?"

"In the scientific sense work is defined as the exercise of force over distance, but I don't think that is what you are looking for," Jennifer answered this time. "I guess it's just what you get paid for," she shrugged.

"I can't think of a clever way for you to figure this one out for yourselves, so I would like you to consider this: think of all the work you do ultimately as a service you perform for others.

"I know," I held up my hand in a "stop" gesture, "you will say that if you are manufacturing a widget that you are producing a product, not a service. Actually, the physical product, in its turn, answers a need for the customer, so again, everything you do is ultimately providing a service. Jennifer, you service your bank customers by providing them with financial products that are in fact intangible services. Susan, you will be servicing your customers, your students, by providing them with education."

"Okay, that makes sense," Jennifer conceded, "but what's the point?"

"If you accept that idea, there is an important point to be made here. Service has an exchange value attached to it in the world. And the rule of thumb is that you always receive rewards in life in direct proportion to the service you provide."

"I get it. So you mean that in whatever job we choose, if we want a raise, for example, as a reward, we have to make sure we are serving our customers and serving them well," Susan explained to herself out loud. "More service creates more reward."

"Exactly."

"I'll bet you now want us to identify what better customer service is," Jennifer anticipated. "Okay, let me see if we can do it as painlessly as possible."

"Is life these days, with Grama and I trying to teach you all this stuff, painful?" I was disconcerted.

"No, Mom. It's just that customer service is one thing I think I already know about," Jennifer consoled.

"All I know is that the customer is always right," Susan put in.

"There's more to it than that, Suz. At the bank we have a four-point customer service policy: Listen,

Respond, Satisfy, Confirm. They teach every employee first of all, to be courteous to the customers, no matter how irate they might be. There is no excuse for bad manners. We listen to the customers in order to identify their needs. After that, we respond to the customers' needs, and again do it cheerfully. We try to satisfy the customers' needs, or explain why we cannot. Finally, we make sure we follow through on any commitments made to the customers, and follow up afterward to make sure they are satisfied," Jennifer said.

"Good," I responded. "In other words, you use the Platinum Rule."

"Don't you mean the Golden Rule, Mom?" Susan asked.

"No. The Golden Rule says: do unto others as you want to be done unto. That's good because it implies you do no harm to anyone. Unfortunately, it also implies that you place your own agenda or values or expectations on others. That may not be what they want. It's sort of like when Aunt Sarah gave you those cross-country skis for Christmas one year, when you really wanted downhill skis. She wanted you to enjoy what she enjoyed. I know you appreciated the gifts but you would have preferred something different. She loves you but she didn't listen to what you wanted."

"Oh, yeah. I see what you mean, Mom," Susan nodded.

"The Platinum Rule says: do unto others as they want or need to be done unto. It implies empathy for someone else's differences and requires understanding their needs.

"That is why the Platinum Rule is the ultimate customer service motto: Listen to the customer. Care about them. Seek to satisfy their needs."

"And never put people on hold," Susan interjected playfully.

"So, to create a general statement, if we reflect back on what Grama said earlier about how you identify quality work, how would you identify quality service?" I asked.

"It would exceed minimum standards of performance or expectations," Jennifer replied.

"Right. Does that make sense?" I asked.

"Yeah, it does," she nodded.

"Good," I praised her. "The only thing we forgot to identify is who the customer is. In this broader service model, it could be the person who walks into the bank to make a transaction. More subtly, though, your customer could also be your boss who has expectations of your performance on the job. Or, in a relationship, your customer is your spouse, someone you serve with understanding and love. In this model, almost everyone can be your customer in some way."

"That's an interesting concept," Jennifer commented.

"Right, and that shift from viewing your customer as a few select people to viewing everyone as your customer creates a new attitude habit where you seek to serve other people. That means living by the Platinum Rule," I summed up. "And, since reward is a function of service, the more people we are serving or the more service we provide, the greater our rewards, and the greater our satisfaction."

"Wait a minute," Jennifer prepared to disagree. "I agree with the Platinum Rule about how to treat other people. But I don't like the idea of 'serving' everyone. That is what women have been forced into for centuries, a subservient position in society! Mom, I'm surprised at you! That mentality doesn't support women!"

"Yeah, Mom!" Susan was preparing to follow suit on this one.

I could have expected this. "Wait a minute. Don't confuse service with subservience. They are two different things. Subservience implies weakness and holding yourself lower than someone else. Whereas service means honoring someone else, everyone else, as your equal. It is honoring the spirit that is in all of us. It goes back to choice—if you choose to serve, you are not being forced into any subservient position. There are no menial jobs unless we allow ourselves to be convinced that what we do has no value. To serve is not a weakness. In fact, it takes a strong and healthy ego to seek first to serve others, before becoming self-serving. Sometimes, it takes a saint. In fact, sometimes it's what makes a saint! It's hard to unselfishly put others ahead of our own ego, and that is why the rewards are also great."

"Okay, I see what you are saying," Jennifer relented.

"The point is, you know perfectly well that I agree with feminism in terms of the fairness of equal pay, and so on, and I'm not saying that injustices have not been perpetrated against women, but maybe now we have to consider another way of seeing life. I think it's time women stopped viewing our social history of being in a serving capacity as something totally negative. The skills and qualities women have by nature and have been encouraged to express and develop—in the area of interpersonal relationships, such as nurturing and empathy—are the skills and qualities that everyone will need to succeed in the next century. You could say that is a positive revisionist view of history but I think it's an optimistic way of choosing to see the waterglass as half full.

"Things have changed. Jen, look at all your business books. The economic model, or ideal, is rapidly moving toward a globalized service model. Good service calls for the best interpersonal communication skills. Companies, and the employees in those companies, are being called on to provide this. Women in business used to be criticized for being too people-oriented. Now the desired model is to be people-oriented. We have the skills, it's time to cash in those chips.

"Don't expect all men to realize or admit it, but their model of future economic success has become the feminine model of human dynamics. Even ecologically, we've found out that we have to work cooperatively, with nature and with each other, in order to survive. It's no surprise that feminism and the ecology movement emerged hand in hand. Both have reached a critical mass in human society. It's a tide that can't be turned back. Men are, knowingly or not, taking lessons from the women in their lives, and the voices of women in society. Yes, there are still some dinosaurs around, and some in powerful positions, but most men have evolved into a much less threatening form."

"Yeah, reptiles," Jennifer wittily replied.

I ignored her joke to continue. "Men know they need to learn from women. It's time to stop beating on men and take the opportunity to teach them, to help them to create the future. Time to shift from the old concept of women as victims to a new vision of women as partners.

"This is my soapbox speech, and I think it's an important idea, so bear with me, girls. I can show you some examples of how things are changing.

"In corporations today, we see fewer of the army-style hierarchy structures with one guy on top of a pyramid of ever-lower minions who have no power to make decisions and take responsibility for their jobs. Now we see organizations where people work in teams."

"Yeah, the bank is like that," Jennifer said.

"Quite the opposite of the old 'top down' rule. We've shifted from a control model of leadership, where employees are just told what to do, to a personal responsibility model, where everyone is empowered to be responsible for their work. This system has proved to be more productive because people feel satisfied and are more motivated when they have responsibility for, and control of, their work.

"Smart companies are now nurturing and sup-porting individual growth and are more compassionate in family matters. Management realizes the company reaps a harvest of loyalty when it plants the seeds of acknowledgment of the individual's contribution and their needs. In management training sessions chief executive officers are taught to lead from their holistic 'right brain' and follow their intuitive gut feelings—a supposed feminine attribute.

"Business courses now teach strategies of coop-eration, or win-win, instead of competition. Look at the language of business even. For years men have used sports or warfare as a metaphor to describe business. Look at all the 'buddy movies' that use playing the game of football or baseball to teach men about the game of life. At best it's a mixed metaphor that teaches the positives of loyalty and teamwork but also the negatives of competitiveness, winner-take-all, grind the other guys into the dust. Well at least that's changing to more neutral examples, like the arts. People who excel are now called peak performers or stars and a manager is seen to orchestrate the department. Work itself is often described as a creative endeavor.

"In medicine, the male doctor-is-in-control model from the seventeenth century is finally returning to the holistic, self-healing model where the patient's body, and spirit, is involved in the healing process. The more we learn about the body and the mind, the more we learn to leave it alone, to trust its ability to self-heal. Healthy self, heal thyself. We've even laid to rest the mistaken stereotype of witches by realizing they were probably just wise natural healers and shamans.

"In my own field of psychology, I constantly see men struggling to regain their lost feelings of humanity, intimacy, and connectedness, the side of their emotions they subjugated for the macho model. Women have always been allowed the complete fullness of our feelings, the joys and the sorrows. We've enjoyed the connectedness that gives us to people we love.

"It's time to reexamine our social history and to see the positives we have gained from it, instead of dwelling on the negatives. That's why it seems crazy to me for women now to operate the way men have in the past—with selfish competitiveness and callous aggressiveness—supposedly in order to succeed. Many men have moved away from that model of success-at-all-costs themselves. Women don't have to stop being women to be successful. It's within this new model that women are able to succeed, and will succeed spectacularly."

"Okay, Mom, take a breath, will you!" Jennifer laughed, and then more soberly added, "I never thought about it that way. Maybe that makes sense." At least she was prepared to consider it. "Service is where we are all heading, men and women, and service requires us to be in touch with people."

"That's right. I'm sorry to put so much emphasis on the subject, but work, or service, takes up more of your time and energy than any other activity. Psychologically, it is deeply linked to our concept of Self. As Freud said, 'the ultimate therapy is work and love.' Work is how we connect with who we are, and how we express our Self. It's one of the major ways we receive affirmation, acceptance, and acknowledgment from others. That's why it's crucial to do work you feel good about."

"In other words, work that is congruent with your values, right?" Susan confirmed.

"That's right. I have one more thing before we get off the subject entirely. Commitment is golden thread number one and builds the value of trust into your character. Goal-setting is golden thread number two and it gives you initiative. Planning is golden thread number three and builds the value of self-discipline into your character. What value does golden thread number four, quality work, build in your character?" I asked.

"Pride?" Susan offered.

"Yes, pride is a part of it," I answered.

"I know," Jennifer said. "Self-respect. No. Self-esteem."

"Right on. Doing quality work builds your inner self-esteem and having high self-esteem makes you do quality work. And around it goes. Don't you just love the way Grama's golden threads seem to be weaving into a complete fabric of life?" I smiled. "You'd think it was all part of a master plan."

"Mother!" they chorused in mock exasperation, and we changed the conversation to other matters.

A master plan indeed. If only life's patchwork quilt always fit together so easily.

Golden Thread #4

Always Do Quality Work

January

Hobbes, That Darn Cat!

*O*nly in television commercials do people sleep
smiling peacefully, with their hair in place,
and wake to the stimulating smell of freshly
brewed coffee, prepared happily and lovingly by
their perfect smiling offspring. I was stimulated
awake this morning to the sound of Jennifer screaming. Oh, no! Was the house on fire? Not quite, not
the house, just Jennifer. She was burning.

"You left the sewing room door open, you
idiot!" Jennifer was screaming at Susan as I fumbled
into my slippers.

"I did not!" yelled the sleepy reply.

"Look at this mess! Look at what you did! That
darn cat! It's all your fault! Look at this mess!"

I had to intercede. I was afraid my typewriter would run out of exclamation marks if the decibels went any higher. By the time I stumbled into the hall-way, Susan was standing in the doorway of the sewing room looking in at Jennifer and a chaos of fabric pieces literally littered everywhere. Some trailed out and down the hall to who knows where. It was the unmistakable work of deft paws. While we slept peacefully and innocently, Hobbes, our rambunctious, nocturnal cat, given the opportunity, had rearranged what had been dozens of neat piles of quilt pieces the evening before, into a total cat-astrophe.

The sight of my two pajama-clad daughters livid among the ruins struck me as sweet and comic and I burst out laughing, which had the opposite effect to what I had hoped for. Instead of diffusing the situa-tion, my hilarity only fanned the flames.

"This is all your fault!" Jennifer bellowed at Susan again.

My daughter bellowing? Before I had a chance to put in a conciliatory "now, now" Susan broke into tears.

"It is not my fault," she sobbed, running back to her room. "You always try to blame me. I hate you!"

Slam!

"It is too! You think you're so perfect. You were sewing last night!" Jennifer yelled at the closed door, then stomped off to her room. "I'm older: I hated you first!"

Slam!

My laughter had given me the hiccups. "Oh, dear," I hiccuped at the mess. "Not one of your wisest motherings," I told myself.

Just then, Hobbes, noise-piqued curiosity, swaggered up to me and sat down, totally unconcerned.

"Merow?" he asked calmly.

"Oh, Hobbes. Now you've done it, buddy," I answered.

Done what? He looked around and blinked. Not a thing was out of place in his opinion. Except maybe this. He reached out his paw to a piece of fabric, deftly flipped it over, and looked at me.

"Exactly," I agreed, and scratched his ears. "Let's have pancakes for breakfast."

Everything lay scattered as it was for two days as both girls studiously ignored their quilts on the floor. Hobbes, of course, rearranged a few more pieces with impunity. We had finally reached the time when everyone knew intervention was looming, so one morning in my best Confucian manner, I taped a note on the refrigerator door that read, "Obstacles do not develop character, they only reveal it."

By the time I had returned home from work, someone had picked up all the pieces and dumped them in a pile in the sewing room. That night I noticed a light on under the door, and the next day found someone else had sorted the pieces back into the two different colored quilt projects, so I did my bit by ironing all the wrinkled and rumpled and chewed pieces again. We were making amends slowly.

Today in the car there was still a sulky silence and then more reheated steam recounting to Grama what had happened.

The girls had chosen their old pattern of being competitive adversaries. Each was holding true to her own worst self. Impetuous as always, Jennifer had not followed Grama's instructions to mark the back of her fabric pieces so her reassembly job seemed insurmountable. Frustration for her always ends in anger and stubbornness. She won't work on it anymore—it can go in the garbage. With the cat. Ever meticulous Susan, on the other hand, had followed instructions, carefully marked each piece and managed to quickly reorganize her work. Still smarting and defensive from Jennifer's anger, she wrapped herself in superior smugness. And there we all sat.

If they were expecting sympathy from Grama, they weren't going to get it.

"Since every upset is an opportunity to learn something," Grama started, "I guess there is some truth to be discovered here. What would that be, girls?"

"I shouldn't have left the door open," Susan finally admitted.

"That's the story of what happened, honey.

What's the truth behind it?" Grama coached again.

"Be more careful," Susan volunteered.

"That's good advice, but no," Grama replied.

"Mark your pattern pieces," Jennifer sighed wearily, acknowledging her error.

"More advice. What is the truth?"

"That things are sent to try us?" Jennifer tried again.

"What things? Sent by whom?" Grama shrugged.

"Okay, then it's not the cat's fault," Jennifer tried another track, resignedly.

"Better," Grama encouraged.

"All right, it's not Susan's fault." Jennifer, again.

"That's the same as not blaming the cat," Grama pointed out.

"It's our own fault," Susan blurted.

"That's still looking to place blame somewhere, isn't it?" Grama asked.

"But it was my fault. I'm responsible!" anguished Susan.

"No! And Yes! No, you are not to blame. Yes, you are responsible. Period. You are response-able. Life is full of unforeseen events. So things happen. You are capable of responding. Only animals react purely by instinct. They are controlled and limited by a stimulus-response process and preprogramming in their brains. But humans are unique in that between the stimulus and the response, or between the event and your reaction, you have a response-ability and can choose your reaction to any stimulus, or event," Grama explained.

"Response-ability is your fifth golden thread to success in life. Your willingness to take responsibility is a measure of the maturity of your character.

"Justifying yourself by blaming others, or worse, blaming yourself, is immature and defeatist. You won't get far in life if you're always looking to blame everything that happens to you on outside factors. Both justification and blame keep you stuck in the past, retelling your woe-is-me story. Accepting responsibility not only cuts off wallowing in destructive self-pity, it opens the door to the future, to learning, improving, and getting on with your life.

"Being responsible means you are in charge. And when you are in charge, you get to make decisions about your life instead of being blown by the winds of chance. As soon as you say, 'I am responsible,' you give yourself choice, the greatest freedom you can have. The most unhappy people I have ever known were those who believed they had no options in life. You always have choices. Sometimes it can be uncomfortable, and it may seem that you're choosing between 'a rock and a hard place,' but you do have a choice. When your grandfather left me to raise five children I could have gone on welfare or gone out to work or put the children in foster homes. None was an ideal solution but I did have a choice, so I went to work. That was something that was looked down upon by most people in those days, but it meant I kept my family together and kept my dignity. It was my responsibility and my choice. Even when you have limited options, having choices gives you independence. Why would you give it up?

"If you willingly accept responsibility your thinking will be clearer, your decisions will be better, and your solutions to any problem will be more creative because you won't be snarled up in useless negative emotions of blame or justification."

Grama finished with, "The more responsibility you are willing to take, the more and greater are the opportunities you are given. Because when you take responsibility for the outcome, you are able to recognize the opportunities and are unafraid to act on them."

I think Jennifer and Susan were surprised. They expected sympathy from their cuddly old grandmother but Grama obviously wasn't going to let them get away with feeling sorry for themselves or let Hobbes be an excuse for quitting. She dismissed the "master class on quilting" part of our visit and sent them home with strong encouragement and a reminder of the fifth golden thread—personal responsibility. She was confident that they would get it all together.

Before we left, Grama showed us the pieces for the quilt top she is working on this year. It's a variation of a Hearts and Roses pattern, one of my favorites. More difficult than a pieced quilt like the girls', each of Grama's blocks would be appliqué work, with some embroidery as well. Slower work for old fingers, but she obviously loved the challenge of it.

I felt a momentary pang when I noticed there among all the pieces were a few hearts cut from Jack's old shirt. I sighed as I let it go and thought, Remember, it's all part of the ebb and flow of life. Everything is here for our use, temporarily, as we ourselves are only here temporally. It felt right that pieces of Jack's shirt, after being worn in joy, then in sorrow, would be passed on to be useful and comforting to another life somewhere. Grama's aged wisdom always makes me feel peaceful and connected. I watch Grama teach the girls about life, and as they respond to her with joyous affection, I'm reminded how lucky we all are.

These are special times and every month I leave reluctantly.

Susan was ready to start sewing her quilt top together. First she would assemble each individual twelve-inch block, then add border sashing, and finally stitch all the blocks into one whole quilt top. For a while there she was in an emotional clear space. For a while.

Jennifer had a tougher time ahead. So much new information was competing with her existing ideas. She had to assess and reevaluate where she was and what she wanted to do. How could she be flexible and come up with a more resourceful solution without losing sight of her objective? Grama had suggested Jen simplify the pattern and replace some of the myriad fiddly-bits with single larger pieces. Narrowing her focus would create something uniquely her own. Time would tell what direction she would take.

Hobbes sat purring happily on my lap this evening as we mused about the day's experiences. No woman is ever a prophet in her own home, they say. Coming from me, I know the girls would have shrugged off this talk about taking responsibility as simply mother-talk. I remember doing the same to my mother.

How come all mothers say the same things, and all kids don't listen? I guess because all mothers sound like know-it-alls. I know mine did right up until I had children of my own and started to sound just like her. It's difficult to accept advice from your parents because when you are young and energetic you lack the patience to listen to experience, and when you are the older and experienced parent you lack the wisdom to guide with quiet patience. That's why grandmothers are so important in our lives. We listen closely to their experience and advice.

Coming from Grama, wisdom down the ages, I knew they would think seriously about it.

Seeds are planted. You never know if they will grow and bloom.

$\mathcal{G}$OLDEN $\mathcal{T}$HREAD #5

Take Responsibility and Be Response-able

FEBRUARY

Stitchin' an' Rippin'

Ll was uncomfortably quiet on the home
front this month. Jennifer had apparently
given up on her quilt for the time being
and Susan was engrossed in schoolwork, although I
suspected that behind her closed door, late at night,
she was quietly stitching away. Hobbes and I referred
to this as "quit quilt" and "quilt on the q.t." For once
I didn't interfere. Besides I knew the imminent visit-
to-Grama deadline would bring some guilt-induced
action: quilt guilt. If they formed a group it could be
called the Guilty Quilt Guild. I'll stop that now.

In the car on the way to Grama's, Jennifer
announced she had a great idea. I was leery.

"Grama said you have to be flexible, right? And

be able to respond creatively to stuff, right?"

I was being sold, and it sounded like it would be swampland.

"Well, I have this great idea. I can take all those quilt pieces and sew them together, crazy-quilt like. That would sort of re-create one whole big piece of material, right? So then, I cut a new jacket out of that. All I'd have to do is buy some lining and buttons and I would have a terrific jacket that would be totally unique and 'me.' Much more practical. I'd get lots more use out of it. Great idea, right?"

"O-o-o, yuk," from Susan.

"Shhh," I shushed her.

I felt like saying to Jennifer, "That's the dumbest, hare-brained thing you've ever come up with," but caught my reaction.

"I'm surprised," I stalled. "Let me think." There are times when a foot simply has to come down. But not now—I was driving the car.

"What do you think Grama will say?" I asked instead.

"Well," she hesitated, knowing full well what Grama would think, and say.

"Exactly," I replied. Jennifer sighed. I continued, "There is a big difference between correcting your course and jumping ship altogether. It's important to be adaptable and able to fine tune your progress according to changing circumstances, as long as you keep heading toward the same goal.

Quitting as soon as difficulties arise, gets you nowhere.

"It seems you are letting this first setback stop you. You need to regain your perspective on this disaster. You know in the future when you can proudly look at your finished quilt, you will realize that this cat-astrophe has passed into history and you will view this as only a minor inconvenience along the way.

"Remember when you broke your leg? At first, it was painful and a big upset. After a while, though, you were able to get around and do things in spite of the awkward cast. In the end, it was really only an inconvenience. Time allows us to change our perspective of events like that. The trick is not to wait for the future to rewrite your attitude. You can decide to take a more objective and philosophical perspective now, can't you?"

"I guess so," she shrugged equably. "I was just trying to take the easy way out, right?"

"Uh-huh," I had to agree.

She was quiet for a few minutes, then, "Grama was right you know. About taking responsibility. It was pretty painful but as I thought about it this past month I realized that if I had followed instructions in the first place and marked my fabric pieces, it wouldn't have been so bad. That made me stop being mad at Susan and Hobbes. I know I was actually mad at myself and I took it out on others who didn't deserve it. That is pretty immature."

I nodded encouragement as she continued.

"When I'm responsible, I'm in control. That makes me feel a lot better," and turning to Susan she said, "I'm sorry I yelled at you, Suz, and blamed you."

"That's okay," Susan shrugged. "I'm sorry I wasn't more careful in closing the cat out of the room. Maybe I could help you sort out all your quilt pieces," she offered in conciliation.

Sisters. They're like kittens that scrap and wrestle and vex each other by biting each other's tails. Eventually, they'll lie down to sleep peacefully curled up around each other. All forgiven. What's the line from the movie? "Love means you never have to say you're sorry." Wrong. Love means you always say you are sorry, are always willing to say you are sorry.

Susan continued mournfully, "Your quilt is going to be so beautiful. Much better than mine. My quilt's going to be terrible. You have to finish yours."

I wondered about Susan's self-deprecating remark but knowing what a fussy perfectionist she can be I assumed she was just being too self-critical as usual. Even the best weatherman sometimes misses storm clouds.

"I wish I had known before about taking responsibility," Jennifer was telling Grama. "When I look back on my life, I could have avoided a lot of hassle and energy-wasting emotion, like you said. And a lot of time."

We had been early and Grama was in the laundry room when we arrived. Jennifer and Susan were now engaged in putting fresh sheets on Grama's bed while she and I folded towels. Why does it seem that so many of our momentous discussions in life take place over such plebeian household tasks, I wondered. Perhaps it's a subtle reminder that we truly live on several levels of existence simultaneously. We are always both physical bodies that need fresh sheets and spiritual entities that seek fresh thoughts and inspiration.

"Unfortunately," Grama commented, "we don't always learn important life lessons in an orderly sequence. Some lessons in life are random, even serendipitous. It is up to us to fit the pieces together, like a crazy quilt. You may actually have heard this message before, you know," Grama smiled and nodded in my direction.

"Sometimes we are just not ready to hear what we are being told or to see what is so obvious to everyone around us. Sometimes people learn the lesson or get the point long after they need it."

"Or never at all," Susan suggested as she stuffed a pillow into its case.

"Right. But wherever you start from, reflecting back from the new knowledge enables us to see how we could have acted differently and prepares us to act better in the future."

"Never too late to teach an old dog a new trick," Jennifer quoted.

"And never too soon to teach us young dogs an old trick either," Susan joked.

"It is healthy and smart to look back, not to dwell unhappily on the mistakes, but in order to learn and to change for the future," Grama repeated. "The most important thing to take responsibility for in your life is learning. You are totally responsible for what, and how, you learn."

With the chores done, we returned to the living room and settled down to talk. For some time everyone had overlooked the fact that Susan brought with her a fat shopping bag obviously full of material, probably her quilt top, until finally Grama asked how everyone's quilting was going.

"Oh, Grama, it's awful," Susan wailed and out it all tumbled. "I just can't do this. I spent hours sewing these blocks and look—the points don't meet, the seams aren't straight, and it's all lumpy!"

Grama picked up each block and examined it carefully. That's my baby, I thought. Where frustration leads Jennifer to anger and kicking out at the world, frustration leads Susan to tears and end-of-the-world anguish, inwardly kicking herself. Two sides of the same coin: blame others and self-blame. Like everything they were learning, the reality of being responsible for themselves would take a while to really sink in and become a habit.

"Everything new takes a while to learn, Susan. It doesn't happen overnight," Grama consoled. "Which of these did you do first? This one. And which was the last? This here. Okay, so let's look at them. Isn't this last one a whole lot better than the first you did? Of course it is. So you can see you are learning and improving with each one, right? You can measure your progress. You can feel good about that, can't you?"

"I guess." Susan pouted, reluctant to give up feeling bad, familiar territory for her. She stopped moping and picked up the last block. Looking at it, she admitted, "I did feel pretty good about this one. Every corner came out even, see?"

"This last one is really good, Suzie-Q," I encouraged her. "Now what would it take to make all the blocks look like this one?"

"Guess I would have to start all over again," she sighed. "But then all this work goes down the drain," she started to whine again.

"Whoa. Then that is just what we'll do," Jennifer ordered. "We can make a start right now. We'll just sit and rip out the seams while we talk today. Come on, Sue, where's your stitch-ripper?" she cajoled. Her own tribulation had passed by a while ago, so she was feeling cheerful again.

"No learning is ever wasted, Susan. I hate to sound like a Grand Old Guru here," said Grama, "but it looks like today's lesson is going to be on learning to learn. And it won't surprise you both to hear that the sixth golden thread is about learning."

"Okay. What's the curriculum, Prof?" Jennifer joked playfully.

As Grama also started to unstitch some of Susan's wayward seams, she continued, "Well, to begin with, you need to understand that learning is a lifelong process. You never really get out of school, or at least you shouldn't ever think you've learned it all. Think of life as a classroom and everything that happens to you is an opportunity to learn."

"So right now, we are enrolled in the basic course, 'Learning for Success 101,'" Susan observed wittily.

"If you like," Grama smiled at the analogy. "The main lessons are these. One: Believe and know that you get better every day. Remember, you can't ever learn less; you can only learn more. Every day you build on yesterday's knowledge and experience."

"Kinda like gathering a ball of string," Susan commented, "or thread I should say."

"Right. That's one of the good things about getting older—every day you know more than you did the day before. At least until you get really old and start forgetting things," Grama joked.

Jennifer added, "But at least you have more to forget."

"Two: Failing is also part of learning. If you never fail, you never learn. When you were little you learned to walk by falling down—a lot. Remember that the only true mistake you can make is not to pick yourself up and try again after you've learned from the failures. Always ask yourself, 'What can I learn from this?' And if you are going to fail, fail big. After all, the harder you fall, the higher you bounce. I remember Edgar Allan Poe once said, 'My personal library has two thousand books in it. Unfortunately, they are all copies of my first book.' He didn't let that first huge failure stop him.

"Three: Every problem or upset is an opportunity to learn. This is sometimes the hardest perspective to take. Life provides everything for your enjoyment or your education. When upsets occur, don't get stuck in the story of what happened, like 'the cat ate my quilt!' Look for the universal truth under it. Then, from the truth, distill out and follow your own wise advice."

Jennifer was nodding thoughtfully. "And isn't that connected to what you said about being personally responsible, Grama? In a sense, I'm the one that's responsible for discerning the truth underneath the events in my life."

"That's right." Grama confirmed her insight before continuing.

"And finally, four: Learning takes time." Grama directed her comments in Susan's direction.

"Yeah, right. Okay, Grama, I get the hint!" Susan replied in mock exasperation.

"As we said, it should take a whole lifetime because there is always more to learn. There will always be times when something is new to you. So be patient with yourself and give yourself time to learn without being judgmental and overly self-critical," Grama concluded.

"That all sounds good," Susan asserted. "That's the important 'what' of lifelong learning. I guess the question that remains is 'how' do you learn properly?"

I picked up the theme to answer, "To begin with, your own life and experience is an excellent direct way to learn. Just pay attention to what goes on inside yourself and around you. Stay alert and observe what happens. Then think about it and what it means. The conclusions that you reach may be as valid and as useful as anyone else's—you don't always have to consult an outside so-called authority for your intelligence or wisdom."

"Are you saying we should just trust our own judgment?" Susan asked in surprise.

"Sure. Why not? You are both smart and capable women, aren't you? In order to be strong and independent thinkers, at some point you have to start trusting your own inner voice."

"And remember to question and continue to reevaluate those conclusions and assumptions that you form," Grama commented. "As long as you keep an open mind, you will continue to learn."

"Makes sense, I guess," Susan nodded.

"And secondly, of course, you can do a lot of

valuable learning by reading," I continued. "That's how you learn from the experiences of others, like you did with the role models we talked about. There is an unbelievably vast amount of knowledge, wisdom, and truth out there in the libraries of the world. Make it a success habit to read every day, not just fluff for entertainment, but books that will improve you, or give you ideas, or stimulate you to think new thoughts. Read books in subjects that you wouldn't normally look at. You never know where a good, new idea will come from."

"But, Mom," Jennifer objected. "No one can possibly read and learn everything in one lifetime."

"Yeah," Susan agreed. "You probably couldn't even read all the book titles in one lifetime."

"No, of course not. The trick to successful reading is simply this: read to teach. Read so that you understand concepts and can explain them clearly to someone else. That's how you'll know you've really grasped the meaning. The details of the data are not important. Anyone can fill in the statistics later. True intelligence is not the ability to memorize huge amounts of facts, but it's the ability to conceptualize, or in other words, to comprehend ideas and communicate them effectively. And it follows, that successful intelligence is the ability to apply those concepts to everyday life," I concluded.

"So always read, or learn, in order to understand, not to memorize," Susan repeated. "Hmmm.

This is something I'm going to have to think more about. As a teacher I'm going to have to teach kids not only the mechanics of how to read, but also how to read, you know, to think."

"That's right," I nodded. "And that may put you at odds with certain aspects of the school system that are geared toward testing and rewarding students purely for what they memorize. That's a challenge you are going to have to face as you move into your teaching career."

Grama drew us back to the present lesson as she concluded, "To come back to today's upset. Susan, sometimes you are too hard on yourself. I know you want to do things perfectly. That's a good success habit—aspiring to perfection. That way you will produce quality work. But you have to temper it with knowing when to be patient with yourself. Don't compromise your intentions or the quality of the work. Just allow yourself time to learn. Which means at the beginning you may fail to meet your own high expectations.

"That is where a lot of people give up. They get frustrated when they don't master or improve fast enough. Don't compare your first quilt with the work of an experienced master quilter. Compare your first quilt with their first quilt. You'll probably be pleasantly surprised to see how many mistakes they too made in the beginning. Give yourself permission to make the necessary mistakes while you learn. That way you will continue on to success.

"Remember, every time you make a mistake, you learn how not to do something. Every time you learn how not to do something, you are closer to succeeding. Remember Thomas Edison. He said he found two thousand ways not to make an electric light bulb before he discovered the right way to make one. Failing leads to success, but only if you learn something from it."

"You're right, Grama. If I could do one block correctly, then I can now do them all that way. I have to keep going. Right? Like you said earlier about being responsible," Susan said thoughtfully.

"Yes. Exactly. Now come give me a big hug," Grama beamed, "and let's get on with it!" Although Susan had started the day downhearted, Grama's sixth golden thread and her comments on learning seemed to really hit home for her and lift her spirits. Anything that applied to the subject of teaching always piqued her interest. These were concepts she could use personally and in her career. Like Jennifer, she too now had to go back a step and redo some of her work.

"While we're on the subject of learning, Grama," Jennifer joined in, "I guess I should now report back, as promised, on what I've learned so far about success."

"Great. We'd love to hear," Grama encouraged her as we all ripped out Susan's wayward seams.

"I'll try to summarize what I think you and Mom have been saying, although it's confusing sometimes. On one hand you can measure success with money and material things like status symbols as some sort of yardstick to tell you how well you are doing relative to everyone else." She raised one hand, palm up, and then the other hand and jiggled them as if balancing invisible weights. "On another hand you can measure success with intangibles like recognition, self-esteem, and generally just feeling good about your accomplishments.

"I get confused though, because success seems to have a lot of choices about it. In both quality, and quantity, depending on your focus—sort of high and narrow or wide and diverse." She again gestured with her hands.

I nodded. "Right. Somewhere I read a quote that said, 'I not only want a long life, but a wide one as well.'"

Jennifer continued, "You can be really expert at one small area, or just reasonably good at a number of things—that's being a specialist versus being a generalist, I suppose. Whatever you choose, there is a cost involved. By choosing one thing, you may have to renounce something else.

"And then again, success can also be just progressively working toward your goal, any goal. That idea really appeals to me.

"In any case, however you define or measure it,

you get success first through your attitudes, then through your actions. A successful attitude comes from your beliefs and values, and is motivated by your reasons for wanting the goal. The more reasons you have, the more motivated you will be. Every action you take toward achieving a goal is important in that it has to support and demonstrate your values. That's the congruency thing. Right?"

Grama nodded yes as she listened.

"It really makes sense, Grama, how your golden threads all work together to create success. You have to have commitment. You have to set goals. You have to plan. Of course, you have to do quality work. You absolutely have to be responsible for your own life. And number six now, you have to make learning a lifelong habit."

Grama grinned happily. "I'm glad you agree."

"Making our quilts really has been like a metaphor for our lives. Whatever fabric of life you choose, these golden threads are the warp and woof fibers that are interwoven to make the fabric. They're the values that weave together to make your character," she concluded.

"That's very poetic," Susan complimented her. She had been respectfully quiet while her sister talked.

"Thanks. One final observation. It seems to me that ultimately the quality of your life equals the combined success of all your choices. The better your choices, the better your life."

"That is excellent." Grama applauded Jennifer's words. "Do you believe everything you said?"

"Yeah," she thought carefully. "Yeah, now that I've thought it through. I guess I really do." Jennifer smiled at the self-revelation and Grama nodded satisfied.

"Then what is confusing?" I asked.

"Okay. It's not the ideas that are confusing, but how do I apply the theory to life? How do you know what career you should set out for? I think I understand the how of success. I'm having trouble with the what. What choices do you make, when there are so many options?"

I patted her shoulder. "Jen, you are not alone in your dilemma. There are so many career opportunities available to people these days, it's difficult to decide. And the fact is, there may be several different occupations that would satisfy your needs and values. That is the wonderful opportunity in our complex society."

"Well, and these days the trend appears to be that people have a series of completely different careers through their lifetime," she groaned.

"That's right, but the trick to career happiness is simply to make sure that in each job you apply the golden threads," I recommended.

"I know you girls hate to be told 'you're young, just wait and things will happen in their own good time,' but you know, more often than not, that is what happens in life," Grama commented. "Like they say, 'you can't push the river,' you have to go with the flow. In other words, you may not know for a long time what your ultimate career is supposed to be and you can't force it. You may have several false starts. You may change your mind. You may have to let it evolve as your needs and interests grow. Don't worry. The important thing is: as long as you are letting your values and genuine interests guide you, you will be okay," Grama advised.

"Yeah, Jen." Susan brightened as she pointedly remarked, "You, too, may have to rip out a few seams and start all over again—stitchin' an' rippin'—until you learn exactly what success is for you. Don't be so hard on yourself," she nudged Jennifer playfully. "Be patient, like me!"

Golden Thread #6

Make Learning a Lifelong Habit

MARCH
Add Zest

*P*eace in the valley this month.

Susan, with her meticulous eye for detail, matched up all of Jennifer's wayward quilt pieces and together they figured out a way to simplify the complex pattern. They replaced some of the small busy-bits with larger patches which resulted in a new cleaner design. Since part of the original fabric had disappeared—gone a-stray-cat you might say—and therefore the whole quilt was going to be smaller, Jennifer decided to invest in a new complementary fabric to add a wide border, making a contrasting framework yet pulling the whole thing together. Necessity, not only the mother of invention, had also produced an attractive solution.

In return, Jennifer continued to help Susan unstitch her blocks in preparation for resewing them together with her newly perfected skill.

Having recommitted themselves to the work, both girls settled down to finish sewing the quilt tops before our next visit to Grama. I think they surprised even themselves with how quickly the work came together for them. There is nothing like encouragement from a sister to rekindle enthusiasm and energy. They discovered that allies and mentors are not only mothers, aunts, grandmothers, and friends, but also sisters. A sister can be a nemesis, but also a growth buddy and helping hand in life.

Despite it all, somehow, we were still on schedule. When we arrived at Grama's we found her peacefully asleep in a comfortable old wing back chair, with her feet on a small tapestry covered footstool. Her hands lay loosely in her lap on her quilt in its small hoop frame, where they must have come to rest as she nodded off. She woke with a start when I touched her shoulder and spoke to her, but she smiled happily when she saw who it was. She adjusted her glasses and set aside her quilting to greet us. The girls couldn't wait to show off so I went to the kitchen to make tea while they unpacked their treasures.

"I am so proud of you," Grama beamed as

Jennifer and Susan held up their now completed quilt tops. "I knew you could do it." Inspecting their work in detail, she proudly hugged them both.

"Excellent. Quality work, both of you. You really worked hard, and despite some setbacks, you came through. Congratulations! You certainly learned a lot.

"I know you both had to step out of your 'comfort zones' and stretch yourselves to get this far and I know that is not always easy," Grama commented.

"But worth it, Grama," Susan said proudly as she folded her quilt top over the back of a chair.

"Did you realize that you were out of your comfort zone? You were because you were both challenged, in different ways, to do something you haven't done before. I guess you could say that is the lesson of the advanced course Learning for Success 201, the sequel that we didn't get to last month.

"It's one thing to learn your lessons from whatever events happen to befall you. But to choose to put yourself out on a limb by actively seeking out opportunities to learn, that is postgraduate thinking. That is being proactive with your life. It's easy to hold on to what you are familiar with. That's your comfort zone, but it can become an emotional trap where you stop growing.

"Whenever you set a goal," Grama continued, "you are choosing to step beyond your present limits, and it feels uncomfortable and intimidating. But that is the only way you find out who you are and all that you can be. Until you set the goal to make a quilt, you didn't know you were capable of learning how to quilt. You can't ride a bicycle until you can ride a bicycle! You will never know how successful you can be unless you set your sights higher than what you think you can do now.

"And that is what adds zest to life. Anticipating failure is usually what stops someone from leaving their familiar comfort zone. When you learn not to let the possibility of failure stop you, you open yourself up to getting out of your comfort zone. Fear and resistance to change keeps people rooted in the status quo. We often confuse that voice of fear we hear in our head as the voice of reason protecting us from harm. It's not true. It doesn't keep us out of trouble—it tries to prevent us from doing anything at all. It isn't logical—it's usually irrational. That kind of anxiety keeps people from challenging themselves and reaching their potential."

The girls had been listening intently.

"But how do we stop fearing failure, Grama?" Susan asked. "Isn't it natural to be apprehensive?"

"Of course, it is. Well, first of all, as we said last month, you have to be aware at the outset that you may fail, in that not everything you do ends in the outcome you set out for. There is always the possibility that you will make mistakes, especially since you've chosen to be a lifelong learner. You can be a beginner any time in life. I was a quilter for twenty years and still called myself a beginner because even though I was good at some patterns and stitches there were many other patterns and new techniques that I didn't know. Just because you are an expert in one area of your life, doesn't mean that you can't be a novice in other areas. If you accept that, emotionally, it takes some pressure off and helps you relax."

"Yeah, let's face it, we all function better when we are relaxed," Jennifer nodded emphatically.

Grama continued, "Remember, making a mistake is not failing. Allow yourself to make mistakes, so that no matter what happens, your ego won't get bent out of shape. Like when you play tennis, in your head always play to win, but be prepared in your heart to lose."

"I understand what you are saying, Grama. But when do you stop feeling afraid? How do you overcome the feeling of fear, or the anticipation of failure?" Susan persisted.

"I think fearing failure usually comes from thinking that failure is bad. But the word failure is simply a label. It's a judgment that we make about an event. Remember when we talked about responsibility? It's the same thing. We can either choose to say this event is a failure, or this event makes me stronger because I have learned. No quilt is ever a failure if the quilter learned something about how to make her next quilt better. No event, in and of itself, is a failure. There is probably nothing that can befall you that has not already happened to someone else who turned it into a success. The only difference was their choice to see it as such," Grama explained.

"The waterglass is half empty," Susan nodded.

"Or half full," Jennifer finished.

"Right," Grama agreed.

"So is it enough to simply change your, um, your attitude, and that makes the fear go away?" Susan asked, somewhat unconvinced.

"I'd like to say so, but the truth is anytime you are out of the comfort zone of what you know, it is natural to be apprehensive of the unknown. The important thing is you can learn to control your fear and not let it control or stop you.

"Here are four simple how-to's in a nutshell:

1. Realize that you are uncomfortable, and why.

2. Then make it okay. Forgive yourself for being uncomfortable. No one is fearless all the time.

3. Decide that your apprehension won't stop you, and get to work.

4. Believe that you will succeed, and know that if you don't, at least you will learn something from the experience. That way you have chosen to make every situation positive."

"What you're saying, Grama, is that you're going to feel fearful, at some time or another, so you might as well go ahead and do it anyway," Jennifer reiterated.

"Yes. And I hate to say it, but the more often you're in these new and daunting situations the more at ease you will feel. That way the threatening unknown becomes the exciting unknown and something to look forward to because no matter what happens you can't lose. You win either way," Grama finished.

"Yeah, Sue, remember when I had such a hard time learning how to swim," Jennifer offered as an example. "I was afraid for a long time to leave the comfort of the shallow end. But my friends in the class were playing pool games and having such a great time that I really wanted to learn. So I eventually had to 'take the plunge.' As I got used to the water and my strokes grew stronger, my fear went away."

"That's a good analogy, Jen," I commented. "When you are stuck on the edge of the pool, so to speak, and you're hesitating to jump in, an easy way to propel yourself forward is to use a little reverse thinking and ask yourself, 'If I don't do this, what good stuff will I lose out on?' The fear of trying something often causes more anxiety than the act itself.

"You see, the most important benefit you receive from challenging yourself is that you eventually overcome self-doubt and your confidence increases dramatically. This is the best positive motivator of all."

Jennifer analyzed this. "Challenging yourself builds courage and when you are courageous and confident you will take on bigger challenges, right? It's another one of those feedbacks."

"So the sixth golden thread is Make Learning a Lifelong Habit, right, Grama?" Susan asked.

Grama nodded. "And the quality of character it builds is confidence."

"Right. Is that a road to success? You bet," I confirmed.

"Here's a thought for you. If failure isn't bad, is success always good?" Grama posed with a twinkle in her eye.

"Oh, no, I don't think I want to hear this!" Jennifer covered her ears laughing.

"I do," Susan said brightly and added her quick inspiration. "Success could be bad if it makes you complacent, so you never leave that comfort zone. Then you never learn anything new. So when things change through time, you don't keep up and you can't cope. What was successful yesterday may not be successful tomorrow."

"That's terrible, Suz," Jennifer declared, having listened anyway in spite of her protestation. "That's almost enough to make me not want to be successful in the first place. Almost, but not quite." She laughed at herself.

"When I'm feeling ill-at-ease," Grama continued, "I remind myself that being uncomfortable is what adds zest to my life, which otherwise could be terribly boring. Like in baking, when a recipe says 'add zest' it means you grate the bitter, and normally inedible, lemon rind into the batter to add some zip to the flavor. Whenever I have a problem I like to think of it as a big juicy lemon. I take a grater and see myself making zest out of it and sprinkling the zesty bits all over. That makes the whole picture sunnier and comical and a lot less forbidding. In other words, it helps if you keep your sense of humor and don't take yourself too seriously.

"After all, God gave us a neck to stick it out!" Grama laughed at herself. "Listen to me, would you? I sure come up with some goofy ideas."

"You always make sense to me, Grama. You remind me of that wise character, Yoda, from *Star Wars* movies. He helped Luke Skywalker become a hero and defeat the powers of darkness," Jennifer teased.

"That would make you our Yoda-Grama. We should call you Yoda-Grama! What a great nickname," Susan laughed.

Quick as a flash Jennifer started to sing a takeoff of the refrain from the song "Cinderella, Rockefella," which sounded so much like what Susan had just said.

"Yo' de Grama. Yo' de Grama that rocks me. Yo' de Grama. Yoda-Grama."

Sometimes she's so sharp it's a wonder she doesn't cut herself. Susan and I joined in the second verse. "Yoda-Grama, Yoda-Grama that rocks me." Grama laughed and shook her head as she started into an impromptu hula dance along with our a cappella serenade.

For the rest of the day, not a lot of quilting work was done. It became a day of lightheartedness and feeling good about reaching a mini-goal along the way. The quilt tops were complete. It was a day of celebration. This work was more important.

Grama had taught Jennifer and Susan the first six golden threads—commitment, goal-setting, planning, quality work, responsibility, and learning. These were all important and serious lessons to learn. Fortunately Grama also made sure they were having fun along the way and were already feeling a sense of accomplishment, acknowledging their achievements so far.

"Lock in the good times!" Jack used to say, closing his fist in a passionate yes! gesture. So often, too often, the tough times are recorded, analyzed, emphasized, and agonized over—far too long. Yet we let the joyous, whimsical times slip ephemerally away, unappreciated.

Like the unseen soft cotton batting used to stuff a quilt, every quilt is filled with hidden memories and stitched with love. I hope that every stitch the girls are taking in their quilt is locking in wonderful memories that will delight and warm them for years to come.

Golden Thread #1

Make a Commitment

Golden Thread #2

Set a Goal

Golden Thread #3

Plan Your Work and Work Your Plan

Golden Thread #4

Always Do Quality Work

Golden Thread #5

Take Responsibility and Be Response-able

Golden Thread #6

Make Learning a Lifelong Habit

APRIL

Sisters

S pring rolled around with its usual mix of late storms and early blooms.

Last month Grama showed the girls the next step in quilting, having them practice by putting her completed Hearts and Roses pattern quilt top together with the backing fabric and batting material. Jennifer and Susan had then been assigned the fairly easy task of preparing their own quilt tops for the final hand quilting. First, they would lightly trace, in pencil, their chosen quilting patterns onto the quilt top. These markings would act as guidelines for the final quilting stitches, the small running stitch that binds all the layers of the quilt together.

Then they would lay the large piece of backing fabric on the floor and add a layer of soft batting material. Finally they would carefully add the quilt top and smooth it out flat. With long running stitches they basted the three layers firmly together in a large grid pattern so the layers wouldn't shift or wrinkle as they worked on them. Some quilters shortcut this step by simply pinning the layers together, but of course Grama insisted that they do it properly the first time to learn how and to avoid headaches—and heartaches—later. This time they *both* cheerfully heeded the warnings of experience and accepted her instructions.

The girls didn't know as we drove to Grama's today that in the trunk of the car was a portable, collapsible quilting frame I had bought for them. They had both persevered to this point and the effort was worth an appropriate reward. And another best tool to reinforce Grama's golden thread on quality work. Little did I realize that this, too, was going to cause Jennifer and Susan further upset and an opportunity to learn a valuable lesson.

On the way to Clareville, Susan asked if we could stop and pick up some flowers for Grama. Susan chuckled mysteriously to herself as she climbed back in the car with her purchase and her secretive grin stayed with us all the way to Clareville. We were able to join in her fun, however, when

Grama unwrapped the flowers: zesty yellow daffodils!

But that wasn't her only surprise.

"I thought about your 'add zest' suggestion, Grama," informed Susan, "and decided to change my quilt. It was too, um, conservative and safe. So what do you think?" She shyly unfolded her work.

We were astonished! Susan had again carefully, and this time secretly, unstitched part of each block and replaced some of her original choice of muted beige pieces with a new sunny yellow fabric. The effect was electrifying. The quilt top now sparkled. It had come alive. What had been safe and pretty was now exciting and unique. She had taken a traditional design and color scheme and made it her own. Even more significantly, she had done it without conferring with anyone. Susan usually likes to hear everyone's opinion before taking action. It's part of her need for security. It also makes decision making difficult for her, when the opinions conflict.

"This is amazing!" Jennifer congratulated Susan and we all remarked about the effect one simple color change had made. It was an excellent example of leverage. Like the word implies, a small push on one side of a lever can have a much larger, dramatic impact on the other side. Wasn't it Newton who said, "Give me a lever long enough, and a place to stand, and I can move the world." A small well-chosen change in Susan's quilt had made a world of difference.

"I really like it better this way," admitted Susan. "I wasn't sure it was going to work out but I had to take the chance. Now, this quilt will always remind me to get out of my comfort zone and add zest. Just like Grama says."

Like the quilt, Susan herself seemed to shine with a new confident determination. She had given herself permission to try. It was probably one of the best lessons she could learn. In the metaphor of her quilt and the feeling it would continue to evoke in her, she had also given herself a graphic reminder to always challenge herself.

We were so excited we had trouble settling down again. But after minutes of exclamation, congratulation, and general "What's new?" talk, Grama suggested they start to work. In order to teach Jennifer and Susan the quilting stitch, Grama had prepared two sample blocks from scraps, in small hand-held lap-sized frames.

"The ideal stitch is small and straight and evenly-spaced," instructed Grama as she demonstrated. "It's as simple as that, though by now it won't surprise you to find that sometimes you have to work very hard to make things simple. That's a paradox of life. It's easy to make things hard and it's hard to make things easy."

While they practiced, I slipped out to the car to retrieve their new quilt frame and then assembled it.

"Okay, there it is." I dusted my hands as I

stepped back from the now-assembled frame. It had only taken me twenty minutes. Fifteen minutes of struggling without reading the instructions and five minutes after reading them. The three all-knowing women of ancient wisdom watched me and shook their heads pityingly. Never mind them. I never follow the manufacturers' instructions. Call it a foible. It was one of those infuriating, endearing quirks that Jack loved to tease me about. It began when we were first married and I tried to change the vacuum cleaner bag and ended up blowing the dirt back out, all over our new carpet.

So Jennifer comes by her rashness naturally, you say. Of course, I could easily do things "by the book" the first time, but I choose not to. It's a way to hold Jack near me, to still feel his tolerant affection. An invisible shirt of comfort that I can still wear.

I must be crazy to admit this.

Fortunately, I can always tell the girls to "follow the teaching not the teacher." After all, we are all imperfect in some way, and we don't always do what is best. If you expect perfection from the teacher in order to validate the teaching, you are bound to be disappointed. And if that leads you to discount or discredit the teaching, you lose the valuable, valid lesson. That's the greatest reassurance a parent has—we can be imperfect and still teach our children well.

"How's it look?" I asked them.

"Perfect," said Susan, obviously humoring me.

"The only problem as I see it," I said, "is we have two quilts and only one frame."

"No problem," said Jennifer as if she had already anticipated this. "We'll just work out a schedule of when each of us gets to use it."

"We can alternate," Susan said cheerfully.

"Okay," I shrugged at Grama. "Whatever you think is best."

"Speaking of problems leads me to ask, what do you know of problem solving in general?" Grama asked.

"A teacher of mine always tells us there are no problems. We should call them 'challenges,'" Susan answered.

"Oh, poppycock!" Grama snorted irritably. "That idea comes from the silly notion that if you merely use positive words in your vocabulary you will find positive, creative solutions. In the air somewhere, I suppose! Trouble is, if you say 'challenge,' but actually feel 'problem,' you are only fooling yourself, and trying to fool others with your fake optimism.

"I prefer not to play that kind of word-game. A problem is a problem. Just that. A problem, like in mathematics, is a question that demands a solution. And by definition, it insists that a solution does exist.

"I believe it is more important to work on your inner belief and attitude toward problems, than to mindlessly change a word in your vocabulary because it's popular to do so. If you believe a positive solution exists for any problem, then you will find it. But you have to have a process to do so. 'Challenges!' Ha!"

Grama was really irked on this one. No one ever said wise old ladies always have to be sweet-tempered.

"Is problem solving a golden thread?" Susan ventured innocently, eager to anticipate the next lesson.

"No, little goose," Grama patted her cheek. "It's just plain old common sense.

"Look. Here's a problem for you," she continued brusquely. "Take this piece of paper, draw nine dots on it like this:

"Now put your pencil on one of the dots. Without lifting the pencil, connect all nine dots using only four straight lines. It can be done," she promised.

The girls did as she told and quickly found themselves stumped. Grama sat back and watched them struggle for a few minutes until they finally gave up. "There now. The solution is this," and she quickly showed them the answer:

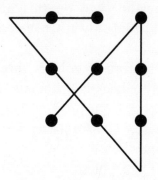

"What happened here is: You gave up. You knew there was a solution because I told you so, but you gave up before you found it. What does that tell you? I don't mean to be hard on you, but this was an uncomplicated little problem. What will happen when you face a really tough problem in life?"

The girls looked chagrined. "Oops!" Jen said.

"The trouble is you assumed that you had to stay inside the square that the dots seemed to form. I didn't tell you to do that. The solution lies in going outside the dots. Solutions to problems often lie outside our assumptions. Assumptions can be fatal to creative solutions, and rigidly holding on to an assumption is absolutely fatal to thinking effectively. So remember, keep an open mind by examining your assumptions and if necessary change your point of view. Getting rid of your preconceptions is the first part of the process."

"Okay, Grama. So I dump all the computer files in my noodle." Jennifer tapped a finger to her temple. "Now that my brain is empty what do I do?"

"People waste too much time focusing on the problem instead of on the solution," Grama replied. "Don't rehash the problem over and over. You should spend twenty percent of your time and energy understanding the problem and eighty percent on the solution. Start by restating the problem in terms of an objective: What do you want to have happen? Then identify the limiting step or resource that creates the problem in the first place. Focus your attention on overcoming that limitation."

"How does that work, Grama? Can you give me an example?" Susan asked.

"No. You give me one," she replied. "Give me a problem. A simple one."

"How about . . . world hunger. Or the diminishing rainforest. Or—"

"I said, something simple," Grama reminded her.

"The problem of where to go to college," I suggested.

"Now state that in terms of an objective," Grama directed Susan, who thought for a moment before replying.

"I want to get the best education possible so I can teach."

"What are the limitations and possible solution?" Grama asked.

"Limitations? Some colleges don't offer bachelor of education programs. Okay, I see. Focus on the possibilities," Susan replied. "How?"

"Ask questions. The problem-solving part of your brain works automatically and will respond to whatever you ask it. Ask the right questions. Ask effective questions. Ask *how* questions, not *why* questions. Why keeps you stuck in recounting the story of what happened. They're static and tend to generate reasons and excuses. You will probably never know the answers to all the why questions you ask in life. Only God knows why. But you can almost always know the answer to how questions. How gets you moving toward an outcome. The answer to a how question is usually an action, and solutions are always active."

"I never thought about it but that's true Grama," Susan commented. "A how question seems to imply that you can do something, it's just a matter of deciding which way."

"That's right," Grama confirmed. "That's why it's a good idea to phrase questions that result in multiple answers, like 'What ways, plural, can I do this?' There is often more than one right answer to a problem. Give yourself permission to be creative and consider alternative right answers until you decide on the one that is most practical for the situation."

"So you don't have to stop thinking just because you came up with the first right answer," I added.

"Like politics," Jennifer observed.

"What do you mean?" Susan asked.

"Well, the whole country faces the same set of social and economic problems, but all the candidates and each party seem to have what they think is the right answer. Maybe the truth is, they are all correct. Each answer would work, if they just stopped arguing, agreed to cooperate, and got to work."

"That's a really good example." I complimented her perception.

Grama nodded. "That's it. After you ask how questions, your brain will storm up some possibilities. So try something. If it doesn't work, try something else."

"See, it's all simple common sense, isn't it?" Grama threw up her hands in resignation. "But of course, like the writer Richard Needham once observed, 'People have a lot of common sense because most people never use theirs up!'"

I stepped in at this point. "Often people stop their flow of creative responses because they think the word 'problem' automatically implies something negative. Remember the problem, like failure, or like any event, is neither benign nor malevolent. It doesn't care if you feel good or bad about a situation.

"It always amuses me to hear people rant and rail about minor incidents in life like getting red lights at intersections. They sound as if the whole world is personally and purposely trying to annoy them. A red light is just an event. A problem is just something that happens. Therefore, you can allow a problem to have a positive or negative impact on you."

"So, be response-able and choose your response," Susan recalled. "It's amazing how responsibility keeps threading its way through everything we do in life. If problems, like failures, are a reflection of the judgments that we make about them, then we can decide to see them as exciting opportunities."

"Right. That's my attitude habit. I choose to see problems as exciting and a chance to be creative," I answered.

"Personally, I always find orneriness helps." Grama now laughed at herself. "I take perverse pleasure in solving a problem, especially one that someone thought I couldn't solve."

Grama and I had agreed to let nature take its course for the next while and watch where it would lead Jennifer and Susan. The first week of scheduling their quilt time proved to be a disaster. There were times when they were both free and wanted time on the quilting frame. Then there were times when each had outside activities and wanted to insist on the other taking a turn. As soon as they had a schedule established, one of them needed to change because of an unexpected conflict.

"Mom, what are we going to do?" Susan wailed as I walked in on a heated debate already underway. As a mother of two daughters I'm used to being called on as a court of last resort.

"We're trying to be efficient like Grama says. A schedule seemed the best answer. But it's not working," Jennifer complained.

"Let's go back to basics," I coached. "What's the problem in terms of your objective?"

"I want to finish my quilt," Jennifer answered.

"And your objective?" I asked Susan.

"Me, too. To finish my quilt," she answered.

"Both quilts, right?" I continued.

"R-r-right," they answered cautiously.

"What is your most important, or limiting, resource?"

"Time to get the work done, I guess," Jennifer suggested.

"And what are all the possible ways of working toward that end? If this one isn't working?" I prompted.

"Try another," Jennifer nodded warily.

"And?" I pushed.

"Focus eighty percent on the solution," Susan recalled.

"Good. Both quilts. Time. Options. See you at dinner," I said as I went to the door.

"Is that all you're going to say?" they demanded, disappointed.

"For now," I promised.

There was laughter coming from the living room when I returned. I found Jennifer and Susan sitting on opposite sides of the quilting frame, both stitching away, looking like Cheshire cats, grinning from ear to ear.

"You guys look pretty pleased with yourselves," I said. "What's up?"

"We came up with the solution. Just like you knew we would." Jennifer laughed. "We realized that we could save a lot of time if we both work on both quilts. We decided we would alternate weeks. We'll leave one quilt on the frame for a week, and whoever has the time, whenever, will work on it. Sometimes it could be both of us at once. Next week we work on the other quilt," she explained.

"It should average out so that we finish both almost together," Susan expanded. "It doesn't matter which quilt we work on. We'll finish both of them. This way we work as a team and we actually save time setting up and taking down a quilt every time we want to do some work."

"Sounds good to me. You came up with a real win-win solution. I'm glad. Cooperation is always a better way," I complimented them.

"What do you mean by 'win-win'?" Susan asked.

"It's a negotiation term," I explained. "Most people go into negotiations with what we call a win-lose mentality. They want to win what they want, which means the other side therefore has to lose. It is competitive and implies that the strongest, or better, side overcomes the other. Trouble is, whoever loses may resent the agreement and end up sabotaging it. This happens all the time in business and politics.

"Win-win is a strategy that sets out to allow both sides to come out even, or better off. When both sides feel they have won, they are more likely to uphold the agreement. It's a cooperative way of operating."

"Like a compromise," Susan observed.

"Right," I confirmed.

"Mom, we thought we were cooperating by coming up with a fair alternating schedule. What was wrong with that?" Jennifer asked.

"You were attempting to cooperate and that means you were far ahead of how most people would deal with the problem. Trouble is, as I see it, each of you started from the premise that your objective was only to finish your own quilt, and you were therefore only prepared to tolerate, somewhat irritably, the other person's objective en route."

"That's pretty selfish," Susan observed.

"Uh-huh," I agreed.

"When you realized the real need was to finish both quilts you were able to consider alternative ideas, like working on each other's quilt, knowing the other person would also work on yours—and all the work would be done," I analyzed. "You used synergy, which meant the combined force of your actions produced a greater result than the sum of your individual forces. You were prepared to make an investment of time and effort in your sister's quilt, knowing she would make an investment in yours. I'm glad to see it because that kind of cooperation, and synergy, only happens when there is trust in each other."

"You mean that we would trust each other to work on each other's quilt and stitch as carefully as on our own?" Susan asked.

"Yes," I nodded.

"But, Mom, we're sisters, who else would we trust," Susan exclaimed.

"Yeah, right," Jennifer agreed.

"Yeah, right, yourself," I declared jokingly. "Aren't you the same two that I left a couple of hours ago in heated debate about whose turn it was to quilt?"

"Yeah, okay, and I think I understand what you mean by synergy," said Jennifer. "But, Mom, why didn't being efficient work?"

"Being efficient," I explained, "works only in relation to yourself and the things you do. You can't make other people efficient unless you expect to program them like machines. When someone else is involved you have to think in terms of effectiveness. When you take all the human factors into consideration, it may not be efficient, but it will be effective.

Effectiveness is how you finally arrive at a result that everyone is happy with. That may take longer, but it's worth it.

"You can take an example from business," I suggested. "For the sake of efficiency, a company may install a computer because it works faster than people. But if that results in people being put out of work, onto social assistance, it isn't an effective long-term solution for society. I'm not against computers or machinery, per se, as long as we remember that people need work for survival. They need meaningful work to give value to their existence. Sometimes we lose sight of the fact that it's people who are important—not the systems.

"In our headlong rush for machinelike efficiency, we have forgotten human effectiveness. You remember, efficiency is always measured against the objective. Like the expression, 'when you are up to your tutu in alligators, it's hard to remember that your objective was to clear the swamp.' We forgot the objective. Efficiency is supposed to make life easier for people. It's supposed to increase the quality of life. If you create the most efficient all-encompassing system to do everything for you, and the people wither away and die spiritually because they have no meaning to their lives, it is all for nought.

"Well, there's another soapbox speech for you— sorry I got carried away again. But to get back to the point of your problem today. I am proud of both of you. You really took to heart what Grama has been teaching you about the first six golden threads of success: commitment, goal-setting, planning, quality work, responsibility, and learning. Up until now, all those lessons have involved your values and growth within yourselves as individuals. I would call that the inner character work. You learn in parallel to each other, but it all took place inside each of you. As you already know, that's where success has to start—in your beliefs and attitudes.

"Because you have two quilts, but only one quilting frame, a new dimension has been added. This was the first time your goal involved interfacing with someone else and called on your interpersonal skills. This is the next step—learning to work with other people. How you behave outwardly with others will always reflect the character you've been building and what you believe in.

"It's too bad Grama isn't here to be part of this discussion. If she were, she would tell you that cooperation is her seventh golden thread. We were talking on the phone last week, and she anticipated what was going to happen to you next. We decided to wait and see if you discovered it for yourselves. And you did. Cooperation is a gentle, more effective way to operate. Cooperation and synergy both mean to work together. An individual can only achieve so much on their own. Ironically, greater successes for an individual are possible through team effort."

"What do you mean, Mom?" Susan prompted.

"Do you remember the 1979 America's Cup sailboat race? Captain Dennis Conner graciously credited the win to the crew. But he wisely chose the right crew in the first place. Because competitive sailing requires split-second coordinated timing of maneuvers, he didn't pick a crew of expert sailors who by nature and training tend to act independently. Instead, he assembled a team of scullers, or rowers, who were trained to row together, to act synchronously for maximum impact. Success went, not to the team of champions, but to the champion team."

"What a great story. Not a team of champions, but a champion team," Jennifer enthused.

"That's right," I continued, "and when you come from the place inside you that believes in cooperation, you will automatically seek win-win solutions."

"Win-win is the ultimate team sport!" Susan exclaimed.

"If we look at it, we can figure what creates a win-win situation. What do you think?" I prompted.

"Obviously, you need a clear objective, where both sides get what they want, or need," Jennifer answered. "We both finish our quilts."

"How do you ensure that the other side also gets what it wants?"

"I guess you'd have to care about them and be

willing to listen to their needs," Susan answered.

"Does that sound familiar at all?"

"Sounds like what we said before about quality customer service," Jennifer suggested.

"Hmmm," I replied nodding and waited.

"Yeah, hmmm," Jennifer smiled and nodded. "Service. All work is service. Service equals reward. Put your customer, everyone, on your team, and go for win-win!" Jennifer made a thumbs-up gesture.

"Terrific. Okay, now how do you ensure that you also get what you want?" I continued.

"Communicate clearly and honestly," she replied.

"Good. Is there anything else that makes win-win possible?"

"Each side would have to agree on the work, on the expectation of performance and results," Susan said, and quickly added, "and agree to work together." She pointed to the quilt. "We have to stitch as carefully on each other's quilt as we do on our own. Like you said, you have to be prepared to make an investment in someone else's outcome."

"Excellent."

"That's right," Jennifer continued. "And knowing we've made a commitment, we can both trust each other to be fair and to also have the other person's interests at heart."

"Bingo! Trust is absolutely crucial. Without trust there is no commitment, and without commitment there is no win-win!" I congratulated them.

"So, we've come full circle back to Grama's first golden thread of commitment," Jennifer remarked. "She said there are twelve golden threads for success. What more can there be?"

"Guess we'll have to wait and see." I smiled what I hoped was a mysterious smile.

They shook their heads and returned to carefully stitching the quilt. I watched them for a few minutes and then observed, "Grama is going to love your old-fashioned solution."

"I thought win-win was the newest buzzword in all the business books. What do you mean, 'old-fashioned'?" Jennifer was surprised.

"Well, look at yourselves. You guys just reinvented the quilting bee!" I laughed.

They looked up from their work at each other stunned and burst out laughing.

"You're right, Mom, just like Grama and the ladies years ago on the farm around the quilting frame. Here we are just sittin' and stitchin'," Susan exclaimed.

"And sharing the workload," Jennifer added.

"And," I continued, "no one ever conducted a time and motion study on them. No one ever taught them management skills. Yet, throughout history women have naturally sought to work cooperatively, to optimize life for everyone, and to enjoy working on a shared goal. Cooperation is an expression of our higher self, our best way of being human. I think women are strongly connected to that principle."

"Pretty clever of them, right?" Jennifer commented.

"Pretty efficient," I intimated.

"Pretty effective!" Susan corrected. We all looked at each other with smirks and then burst out laughing.

Golden Thread #7

Cooperate

MAY

Yes, She Can

$\mathcal{I}$ don't know if it was simply the energy of late spring and the joy of warm weather coming that kept my quilting bees buzzing. Jennifer and Susan were actually enjoying their work, despite pricked fingers and sore shoulders. I often saw them sitting quilting alone with the television or radio playing, Jennifer's pop music and Susan's Mozart.

Just as often, though, I found the two of them at the quilting frame rooted to the commonality of the work. I also overheard bits of conversation, laughter, debates on rock versus classical music, men, and so on. Face-to-face, as it were, for hours at a time, they couldn't avoid talking to each other.

Strangely, they were actually communicating

with each other—listening, debating, trying to understand, laughing, enjoying, and learning from the differences, delightfully surprised by what they found out about the stranger who was their own sister. Taking a page from their problem-solving lesson, they had dropped their preconceptions about each other, and had opened their hearts to seeing their sister's reality.

I was reminded of Buckminster Fuller's theory of precession, which roughly states that often as we proceed through life in one direction toward an avowed goal, our real purpose in fact may lie undiscovered at right angles to our course without our being aware of it. The example of the honey bee, appropriately, comes to mind. The bee travels to the flower, or goal, with the intention of making honey. However, in the grand scheme of things her true purpose may actually be to cross-pollinate flowers. The bee does not know that. Discovering our true purpose can be a lifetime challenge. We, too, may be moving from flower to flower, thinking we have only ourselves to worry about when in fact we are constantly planting seeds, creating a garden. We need only look over our shoulder to see the blooms.

Jennifer and Susan received the unexpected gift of getting to know each other, as a right-angled byproduct of their apparent objective to simply finish their quilts. By applying themselves to the work, they reaped benefits "unforeseen in common hours," as Emerson wrote.

*

"Susan is going to be a great teacher," Jennifer said emphatically. "Mom, I have to tell you and Grama what happened last Saturday. Susan was baby-sitting Lisabeth. Grama, that's our neighbor, Mrs. Martelli's, four-and-a-half-year-old daughter. When I came home, I found the two of them in the living room sitting at the quilt rack. Lizzie was propped up on a telephone book. 'Watcha doin'?' I asked, and Susan answered, 'Lizzie's helping me quilt.' 'She can't quilt. She can't even sew,' says I. 'Yes, she can. Look,' says Susan and then explained that Lizzie wanted to help so Sue taught her to thread the needles she was using. Under a watchful eye, of course. It took her a long time to thread one but you know how focused a four-year-old can be. By the time Lizzie threaded one needle, Sue was ready for it. Lizzie pointed to 'her' stitches where 'her' thread was and she was a proud little girl, I tell you. Isn't that neat?" Jennifer finished.

"It sure is. And it's so true," Grama replied. "There is a way for everyone to contribute. Sometimes it takes creative thinking to find a way but there is always a part for everyone to play.

"Again, if you think about your quilt project, there are many different components that are all important to the whole. The quilt top is artistic and attractive and gives eye-appeal. The backing provides sturdiness. Even between the layers, the invisible batting provides a necessary quality of heat retention. The quilting stitches hold everything together and provide the definition of a quilt.

"And so it is with people. Everyone has a part to play. Even the invisible task or backstage parts are necessary to the whole. So there are small tasks for the little ones and bigger tasks for the big people.

"You see, making a contribution is a way of feeling that we belong. We all need to feel that we are a part of something, that we matter. The person who contributes feels good, feels important and necessary. They feel connected. Like the Bible says, it is more blessed to give than to receive, if you read 'blessed' as meaning it feels better.

"Making a difference is how we create a sense of purpose in our lives."

"So, making a contribution—Contribute and Make a Difference—could be golden thread number eight, right?" Susan anticipated.

"That's right," Grama continued. "You can contribute on many levels. The more successful you are, in terms of accomplishment, the more you are able, and should, contribute. When we succeed at anything we are obliged to turn around and give back, in some way, to help someone else succeed.

"This is the concept of tithing. It doesn't just mean giving money to a church or charity. It means working in a way that ensures everyone else also succeeds. Making a contribution to society through our work and making a difference in people's lives through our relationships is the way we pay back for the success and abundance we have received.

"Contribution is service, or work, at the highest level. Remember that we receive rewards in life in proportion to the service we give. To look at it another way, service is the price we pay for the room we occupy in life," she concluded.

Jen was quiet, a thoughtful but unnatural reaction for her. I could almost hear her thinking this was too much like evangelical poverty. I imagine that she perceives the dilemma as: do I pursue money and worldly success or do I pursue a meaningful, and possibly unpaid, peace of mind?

Susan is lucky. She is one of those fortunate people who has always known what she wants to do. She wants to teach. She is the thought-full one who has always had a quiet sense of purpose. I've had other concerns for Susan because she is so quiet and shy and lacks self-confidence in social situations outside the safety of our family circle, but I've never had to worry about her convictions and direction in life.

Jennifer, on the other hand, is the family's squeaky hinge and therefore sometimes receives a disproportionate share of oil and attention, and "air-time." She has struggled with her direction for years, changing her mind many times. Career enthusiasms often turn out to be flavor-of-the-month whims. For a child of her generation, success in the form of quick money and power is the superficial lure. Quieter moments of introspective discussion reveal the deeper value-driven foundation of her character which struggles to reconcile with her "stuff goals." Many late-night gab sessions have revealed these ambiguous, apparently mutually exclusive desires.

As I turned back to the conversation, Grama was continuing her thoughts.

"You know the expression, what goes around, comes around?" The girls nodded yes. "It has a sort of revenge connotation to it, doesn't it? It suggests that we will reap what we sow. But I think it also has a deeper meaning. I sincerely believe that life cooperates with good endeavors. The more you give, the more you receive, and the more you have to give."

Grama left them with that thought for a minute and then continued, "Most of what we do in life, we do for ourselves. We're busy working for a living, raising a family, making friends, working out, taking holidays, and on it goes. Contribution is how we strike a balance by being selfless. Everything needs a balance. Light and dark. Summer and winter. Yin and yang. For all the selfish pursuits we have, we need a selfless counterweight. That's how life stays in balance."

"You see, Jen, you may find that it isn't a simple and/or situation after all," I suggested. "You are not necessarily condemned to choosing between a purposeful life and a comfortable life or between meaningfulness and materialism."

"But how can the two be reconciled?" she struggled.

"Think about your quilt again," I explained. "Think, if you will, about the essence of quiltness. A quilt has a purpose, right? It can serve the useful function on a bed of keeping a person warm. A quilt also has an aesthetic, eye-pleasing aspect through its external material design. The two aspects are interwoven and balanced.

"If you remove purpose from the quilt, or from life, you are left with artifice and no substance. If you remove the pleasurable aesthetic quality from your quilt, or life, it becomes flat, colorless, without spirit or emotive power. Does that make sense to you?"

Jennifer nodded slowly. "I think I understand what you are saying. I have to design goals for my life that take both into consideration. I need to do work that has value or purpose by making a difference. Yet it should also be work that I enjoy and that uses my talents." Again, she nodded thoughtfully. "I like the idea that success is the process of working toward a goal, not the goal itself, and that it's okay to want the stuff too."

I nodded.

"If I understand what you and Grama are saying, I need to structure my career goals, and in fact my life goals, around making a difference, not around making money. The rewards will come naturally from my service if I am doing what is right, according to my values, my interests, and my talents. That creates congruency between my actions and my values which is the key to happiness, success, and peace of mind. I can balance purpose and pleasure," she nodded finally with satisfaction.

"Right! That's the way to start," I encouraged her.

"Great. Now I have the how all stitched up. I just have to figure out the details of what," she said with a smile.

A few weeks later Jennifer came to me. "Mom, I'd like to know what you think about the new goals I set."

"Terrific! Tell me about them."

"Well." She paused and took a breath. "Okay, we talked about some possible plans and I've decided to ask for that transfer to the Customer Services Department. Within five years I want to become the Customer Services Manager. I know, you are going to ask why do I want to be the manager and you are thinking it's for a big salary, the status and everything. That is part of it, but the other reason is so that I can train people in good customer service. I can make a difference that way. I really do enjoy helping people and I think I'm good at it.

"I also thought I would offer a course on basic financial planning at the local high school, to teach and pass on some of the stuff I've learned. To make a contribution." She was embarrassed. "Does that sound too noble?"

"Sounds a lot better than making a million dollars just so you can buy a ranch in Colorado," I assured her. "I think your goal sounds fine and anything I can do to help, let me know."

"Well, I would like to hear what you think of my five-year plan. There are some courses I need to take and management skills I have to acquire. Here, I have it all written out." She pulled the papers from her handbag. "I keep it with me, to remind me."

"And a plan, too! I'm impressed!" I hugged her and we sat down to discuss the details of her new life plan.

Some chicks fall from the nest, some jump. Either way, they fly or die.

GOLDEN THREAD #8

Contribute and Make a Difference

JUNE
Boredom Sets In

For weeks now my "bees" have buzzed away on the two quilts. At first they found time every day, even if only a few minutes and the work proceeded apace. Their initial concentration on mastering the quilting stitch quickly paid off as their stitches became smaller and straighter and evenly spaced. They were pleased with their new skill and with the results as the subtle quilt patterns spread over the quilt. They were soon able to work faster and the sewing motion became natural and automatic.

After a while it no longer took the same concentration, and as you can imagine, their interest began to wane. The expanse of surface space yet to be quilted ironically seemed to loom larger. Space and time are all relative. Einstein once explained the relativity of time this way: an hour spent talking with a pretty girl can seem as brief as a minute, but a minute spent sitting on a hot stove can seem like an eternity. Their project became a burdensome task because boredom had set in. Disinterested in the tedium of the now repetitive work, they spent less time at it, and progress slowed down.

"So, how is the quilting going, girls?" Grama cheerfully asked this afternoon as we washed and dried the lunch dishes. It had been obvious during our visit over lunch that Jennifer and Susan had studiously avoided the subject until Grama brought it up.

"Fine" and "just great" they replied equally cheerfully.

"Uh-huh." Grama nodded suspiciously. "Any problems at all?" she asked casually, as she put plastic wrap over the leftovers and placed them in the refrigerator.

"No. Everything is fine, right, Sue? We're just working away. There is still lots to do, of course," Jennifer "chirped" "pertly." We hate those words.

"Uh-huh." Grama again, eyeing them closely. "So you're enjoying the quilting?" She leaned against the fridge door with her arms crossed.

"Oh, of course, Grama. Everything is fine," said Susan.

"Uh-huh," Grama repeated. "Okay. You've done your duty at making an old lady feel better. Now tell me the truth. I always know, Susan, when you say everything is fine and your voice goes up an octave that something is wrong. What is it?" Grama demanded.

"Well," Susan hesitated, putting the last plate in the cupboard.

Jennifer jumped in. "Grama, it's just so boring." She slapped the dishcloth into the soapy water peevishly. "It's the same thing over and over again. It feels like this will go on forever. We are never going to finish!"

"And you, Susan?" Grama nudged.

"I'm sorry, Grama, but it is pretty boring. And it gives me a sore shoulder."

"I don't know how anyone makes it through their first quilt, much less a second or more," Jennifer exclaimed. She's never been good at long-term projects. "No offense, Grama, but why would anyone make a second quilt?" Susan hung up her towel and Jennifer let the water out of the sink.

Grama smiled.

"You won't know the answer to why until you finish your first one and can stand back and look at your work. If you fall in love with it, you'll forget the pain and boredom and you'll make another one. But in the meantime, it looks like we need the p-medicine for two girls with p-moan-ia! What dosage do you figure?" she asked, turning to me.

"Oh, they've got it bad. A double dose at least." I smiled. Grama leaned on my arm as she and I walked slowly out to the living room. The girls followed.

"What? What is p-medicine?" they puzzled.

"Girls, at some point every job becomes routine no matter how much you love it," Grama explained as she settled into her favorite chair. "Even the most glamorous occupation or exciting project has drudgery bits. There's no getting around it. The only solution is to remember the formula for p-medicine: equal portions of your positive p-words: patience, perfection, persistence, perseverance, and pride.

"No doubt about it. Quilting takes a lot of time, so be *patient*. The best things in life, and great works, don't happen overnight. Any kind of success takes patience. You better learn it now. If you're not good at waiting things out, start practicing. And that doesn't mean going away and returning when you think the dust has settled; it means staying focused while you wait and work.

"Remember, *perfection* is your goal and it takes hard work. Sometimes you simply have to bear down and get it done. That phrase comes from childbirth where you bear down until you get results or perish! *Persistence* connotes a sense of stubborn determination that you need to see it through, and *perseverance* means to continue in spite of the difficulty you encounter along the way. Then, last but not least, take pride in not quitting or admitting defeat."

"Patience, perfection, persistence, perseverance, and pride," Susan repeated and counted them off on her fingers.

"You see, the p-medicine is a sort of 'magic elixir' that builds your endurance. Having enough stamina means that you will survive long enough to reach the finish line. Too often people give up just a few steps from success. Don't let anyone dissuade you. Grandma Moses took up painting at sixty-five and they told her 'you can't paint' but she went ahead anyway. If you just hang in there, your goal may be right around the corner," Grama explained.

"The only way to fulfill your destiny in life," she continued, "is to reach that finish line, by persevering to the end. That's what sets leaders apart from the could-have-beens. It's how you set an example for those that follow after you. That's how you can influence and have an impact on others—by showing them a completed quilt, a realized possibility, not a half-finished one."

"Wow, I like that," Jennifer enthused. "So next time I'm suffering from boredom, I'll stand up and yell, 'I've got p-moan-ia!'" she laughed.

"Then just sit down and continue working anyway?" Susan questioned with a shrug.

I stepped in then with, "There are a lot of positive actions you can take to feel better and help yourself cope with boredom and the down times. First, when you are faced with something arduous that you are required to do, simply decide to make it a goal. In other words, consciously choose to do it."

"What you are saying," Jennifer interrupted, "is, again, be responsible and actively determine to do it."

"Exactly," Grama confirmed. "Always remember you are doing something because you want to do it. Nobody forces you, except you. You wanted to make the quilt in the first place. Try to remember your original enthusiasm and excitement, and recall how you initially saw the finished quilt in your mind's eye and then think of how great you will feel when you finish the quilt."

"Remember when we were talking about planning, and we said the only way to eat an elephant is one bite at a time? Well, another strategy you can use," I suggested, "is to break that long and seemingly unending task into smaller ones. Make it a mini-goal to do just a little bit, say, one block every two weeks. You'll feel that you're making more progress that way, than if you are always comparing what you've done to the whole lot left to do."

"That's right," Grama agreed. "Every little stitch appears insignificant in itself, but added up makes a quilt. The little everyday acts you do add up to a lifetime—they add up to success. Life is cumulative and every little stitch counts.

"Something else you can do is interrupt the pattern," Grama continued. "Go out and do something totally different, and you will come back refreshed. If you are bored with reading, go exercise. If you are bored with exercise, go read. The point is do something that uses different parts of your body and brain.

"And another really important thing you can do is get out around people. I know it sounds weird, but believe me, failure and giving up too soon often comes from isolation. When you wrestle with a dragon alone, it seems to grow bigger all the time, to the point where you stop fighting. Go talk with people. Share your problems. Tell them what you are doing, and why, and you will hear your enthusiasm increase automatically as you recapture your purpose. You may even find that they've faced similar dragons.

"Needless to say, you need to talk with positive, supportive people who will reenergize you. And your enthusiasm, in turn, will energize them. Stay away from negative people who try to steal your enthusiasm. You won't change them into positive people, but they will drag you down to their unhappy level. That's what 'misery loves company' means. Miserable people want you to join them in their misery."

"At school we call them the moan-and-groan society," Susan added. "They can always give you tons of reasons why you will fail."

"Don't listen to them," Grama warned. "Negative people need to measure themselves relative to others. It's only by grinding someone down that they can feel superior. Remember, if your friends aren't successful and happy, don't take their advice.

"Which brings me to today's surprise." Grama redirected the conversation. "I had a feeling by now you girls would be bored with quilting. This is the part where the glamour of making a quilt usually wears off because all the exciting planning and learning are over. Quilting is exciting and challenging. Let's face it, it can also be time-consuming and boring."

Grama continued, "It's all well and good to be positive and have proactive plans and intentions. It's relatively easy to make plans. It's also human nature at times to feel lousy and unmotivated when faced with the reality of the work. To deny these feelings is foolish. It's okay to be bored, girls, but do something about it. It's like we said about calling a problem a challenge."

"I'll never make that mistake again," Susan exclaimed.

"Therefore," Grama continued as if she hadn't been interrupted, "it's essential to have fall-back strategies, like the ones we discussed, to help yourself through those times. And, amazingly enough, the ninth golden thread is Persevere Through the Tough Times. Know how to cope with the unpleasant side of life."

"If I didn't know better, Grama, I'd think you were just making these up as you go along," Jennifer exclaimed. "You always seem to know what is going to happen to us next."

"Maybe she's been there before too," I suggested.

Susan hadn't listened to Jennifer's comment. She was still thinking about Grama's latest golden thread. She brightened up then with a look of inspiration on her face.

"It seems to me that the more self-confident you are, the better you are able to cope. And the more you know you are able to cope, the more self-confidence you have," she summarized the point of the lesson.

"That's excellent," I complimented her.

"See, we're getting better at this stuff. You could almost say that there is a 'thread' running through our lives now!" Jennifer joked, and Grama threw a pillow at her playfully.

"As I was saying," Grama continued with mock exasperation. "The Clareville Quilt Guild is having a quilt show this weekend and I bought tickets for us to attend. After that terrible pun it is obvious that you need to air out your brains. Miss Stanton will be here at two o'clock with a wheelchair for me so that we can zip around the show easier. In the meantime, girls, let's do lunch!"

I thought the wheelchair was an excellent idea. No point tiring old bones more than necessary. Besides, Grama had trouble walking recently. Her enthusiasm for the girls and their quilts was as strong as ever but she seemed to be moving slower and with deliberate concentration and effort. I know that if she were in pain she wouldn't complain. She always denies the limitations of her age. Yet I noticed on her own quilt frame that progress had slowed to a crawl.

Perhaps she, too, was finally tired of the project. Having made so many quilts, how could she continue to be interested and find meaning? Silly question. Grama would always find meaning in her work because she would give meaning to the work. Perhaps she was just tired and I was worrying too much. The outing to the quilt show would do us all some good.

On the drive to the show I recounted to Jennifer and Susan my experiences of going to the quilt guild meetings years ago with Grama and her friends. I wasn't a member but it was fun to go along once in a while to observe how all the other women tackled their projects. It was a study in human psychology and the patterns of behavior that led to joy or heartache.

Some women went year after year to every workshop and were continually starting a new quilt block pattern, starting some new project, yet never sewing all the blocks together and never finishing anything. Other women sewed lots of quilt tops but didn't assemble them into quilts. They would spend all the long hours sewing and correcting until they had a perfect quilt top, then they would fold it away in a drawer, unquilted, while their enthusiasm carried them off on another project.

It was sad to see those women toil so hard, and deny themselves the satisfaction of completion before moving on. Quiltus interruptus does not satisfy. At show-and-tell nights, they sat wistful and envious of the beautiful complete quilts on display, and promised themselves, yet again, to finish the next quilt for sure.

There were women who would attend a workshop where the instructor carefully taught a new block pattern. Then they hurried home to throw it all together in a race to be the first one back with a finished quilt. Sometimes it would have uneven corners, points that didn't meet, large uneven stitches, or any other sign of hasty careless work. Yet the other ladies would all compassionately applaud her effort, and dutifully congratulate her on her speediness—what else was there to praise—while silently feeling a sad disapproval of poor workmanship. Once in a while a more experienced member would offer gentle, helpful suggestions which more often than not went unheeded, if not unheard.

There were women who struggled mightily and who could make the simplest pattern into a major battleground of frustration and defeat. While one would give up, saying, "See, I can't do anything," her soul-sister would continue to fight every step of the way, struggling hard but always missing the ease of mastery. Both choosing to reinforce their "life is a struggle" mentality for themselves.

Of course the expert needlewomen were expert because "they were taught very young" or "they have no children, or a spouse, or career to take their time," or "they were born with talent," or "they were just plain lucky."

It amazed me how many reasons for success were ascribed to the experts, who took none on for themselves. The expert quilters were simply women who continually learned about their craft, progressively challenged themselves and carefully applied themselves to both the grandness and the drudgery of the work. And when it was all done, they quietly stood in the limelight, with satisfaction, savoring the moments of accomplishment before turning to guide and teach the younger women.

Jennifer and Susan had no preconception of what an impact the large community hall full of quilts would have on them. They were astonished by what they saw in the quilt show. Dozens of quilts. Huge queen-sized ones down to small wall-hanging size. Every quilt was displayed fully flat, either hung on a wall or suspended vertically from large frames, aisle after aisle, like giant paintings in a gallery. And like an immense museum of art there were styles from traditional to ultramodern. Moods from cheerful to somber, from elegant to whimsical. A kaleidoscope of emotions, colors, tones, and hues to shame a rainbow. An exuberance of Life!

Grama happily guided the girls through the show, pointing out design details and commenting on levels of expertise. In one section we found the entries in a Challenge Quilt competition. Grama explained that every quilter had been given identical sets of four different fabrics. Their challenge had been to make a quilt that measured a certain size. The design was their choice, and they could add up to two other fabrics. The resulting twenty quilts, although containing the same common ingredients, were totally unique and different according to the added creativity of the individual quilters.

"This is fascinating, Grama!" Jennifer was suddenly wide-eyed with revelation. "Every one of the quilts is the same, yet every one is different. Each one is a unique combination of the same ingredients. And every one is beautiful! This is so right. It's just like you said a long time ago about people—value and celebrate the difference!"

As had happened to Susan with the zesty yellow additions to her quilt, we could see Jennifer was having one of those aha! reactions that was locking in a lesson that until now was only a concept that sounded right but had no realization. The most memorable lessons we learn in life are the ones that come to us as compelling metaphors with powerful images. Jennifer now had a metaphor that would always remind her to see the differences in people as complementary and valuable. I hoped that tolerance and understanding would continue to mature into the wisdom she is so capable of.

As we continued on, we noticed there were several guild members in attendance, all wearing white gloves in order to handle the quilts with care and respect. Each guide was happy to talk about quilting with Jennifer and Susan. They shared their experiences—many of the same problems the girls had been through. Hobbes wasn't the only cat to dismantle hours of work. And although many women said they truly enjoyed the hand quilting itself, they nodded at Jennifer and Susan with true understanding, acknowledging the backbreaking tedium of it at times. Yet every woman said the lasting satisfaction they felt at completing the quilt far outweighed their discomfort.

Was this a message they needed to hear? You bet.

Occasionally one of the guild members would carefully turn back a quilt to reveal a different and sometimes elaborate pattern on the reverse side. As we examined one particularly stunning quilt, Jennifer puzzled, "Why would anyone go to the trouble of putting designs on the back that no one will ever see?"

"Maybe to make it reversible?" Susan suggested a practical answer.

"How about pride of workmanship?" I suggested.

"Edge," Grama commented quietly. The girls looked at her curiously so she elaborated. "Do you remember we talked about quality work? You can coast through life by just meeting the minimum standards of performance. But quality work always exceeds customer expectations, even if it is simply to add a smile. It's called 'added value' and that's what gives you, or a company, an edge on the competition.

"Is this a successful quilt? Is this the work of an expert needlewoman?" Grama asked.

"Sure," Susan replied, happy to display her new discriminating skill. "Look at the fine, even stitches and detailed, intricate design."

"Could the front of this quilt succeed by itself as a model of quality work?" Grama pursued.

"Sure," they nodded.

"The quilter didn't have to put anything else into it, did she? She chose to do so. She chose to exceed expectations, to go an extra mile for her customers, the user or viewer. That gave her an extra edge, a winning edge, an edge for success. Remember that. In a room full of accomplished and beautiful quilts, this one is truly outstanding.

"Our golden thread number nine was Persevere Through the Tough Times. And this is an example of the kind of results you can achieve when you do," she concluded.

We discovered that the woman who made the quilt was present and Jennifer and Susan were especially anxious to talk with her. They were effusive and sincere in their compliments and she just smiled sweetly, saying "thank you" graciously.

Their burning question was, how long did it take her to complete the masterpiece? How long had she struggled?

"People always want to know how long it takes to make a quilt. Every beginner wants to know what they're getting themselves into. The answer is, it varies. Like life. For some it's quick and easy, for others it's a long, long process. Depends on how much else you are doing, how focused you are. I work full-time and I have three teenage boys. This quilt took me nine years," she smiled anticipating their reaction.

"*Nine* years!" Susan exclaimed.

"Nine *years*!" Jennifer whistled.

After we dropped Grama at her apartment, all the way home Jennifer and Susan relived their astonishment. They were inspired by the artistry and creativity of the quilters they met. They were also challenged and somewhat intimidated by the spectacular quilts they saw on display. Talk about changing their perspective. The quilt show had obviously been exactly what they needed.

Today had been a lesson reinforced by a potent emotional experience. Grama's ninth golden thread, Persevere Through the Tough Times, was a lesson they would not easily forget.

The girls had needed to get out around people, as Grama said, particularly a group of positive accomplished women who "spoke" encouragement through their work and through the example they set.

Leave it to Yoda-Grama to know.

Golden Thread #9

Persevere Through the Tough Times

JULY
Pigs Can't Fly

*J*ennifer and Susan slowly and steadily pro-
gressed through their quilting. Every once in
a while I would hear someone yell, "I have
p-moan-ia!" and out she would go, to the movies, or
to play tennis. A while later, having broken the pattern, she would be back quilting again.

Grama hasn't been feeling well lately, and she
called a couple of times to postpone our monthly
visit. Nothing to worry about, she said. She was "just
feeling lousy and not up to visiting." But let's face it,
she's eighty-five, and we worry.

As things turned out it was probably for the better. The girls were even busier than usual with their
summer activities. Susan's summer job is teaching

crafts and games to children. You might know, by the second week, one of their projects became a quilt to hang on the classroom wall. They used large brightly-colored scraps from their mothers' sewing baskets and chunky, easy-to-handle yarn.

Here was Susan, who had not completed her own apprenticeship with Grama, already starting to pass on her knowledge to her young students. An unintentional reminder that, in fact, we do not need to graduate before we have something valuable to teach and give.

Naturally, Susan talked with the children as they worked on the quilt, and out of that came an idea to write a series of funny stories, teaching them Grama's golden threads in a simple child-appealing way. We've had lots of fun at the dinner table kicking around ideas. The first story she wrote is called "Pigs Can't Fly," which is about a little girl on a farm and her pet pig. We think it's a real "squeal." Now she needs to find an illustrator and publisher, of course.

So far, Jennifer is happy with her customer service job. The other day she came home with a new challenge. She has to prepare a twenty-minute presentation in her management training course. It's been a long time since she made any speeches in high school, so she came to Susan and me, her team, for help. Together we brainstormed some ideas while we sat around the old kitchen table that's been the site of many family powwows over the years.

"Of course, the essence of any presentation is communication, so let's be clear about the basics of communication first," I suggested.

"You want to talk about talking?" Jennifer smiled. "I thought we already did too much of that."

"Well, that may be true but there is more to it than that, of course. I think the important point, even in a supposed one-way communication where you, the speaker, make a presentation to someone else, a listener, is that you have to assess your audience and speak accordingly. A presentation is never truly just one-way. Any time you stand up to speak, there will be a response, whether it's expressed openly or not. As the speaker, you are responsible for the reactions you create in the other person, or people. In other words, you are responsible for the response you receive from them."

Jennifer analyzed that. "So you have to know who you are talking to before you talk."

"So don't talk to engineers about cooking or cooks about engineering," Susan joked.

"I think Mom means more than that, Sue. She means if you talk to engineers about cooking you are responsible for their reaction. You better be prepared for their response, for them to be bored or annoyed."

"Or hungry," Susan said under her breath, continuing in her playful mood.

"Right. Well put," I directed to Jennifer. "The first half of communication is understanding your audience. I've heard it described as, 'seek first to understand, then seek to be understood.' No one listens until they are heard. Your first intention should be to find out who your audience is. What are their goals and interests? What do they need to hear from you?"

"That sounds like customer service," Jennifer realized.

"Exactly," I continued. "The second part of communication is presentation techniques that will improve the effectiveness of your communication. If you stop joking around, Susan, you can probably help Jennifer here with some ideas from your public speaking classes."

Susan sighed and nodded. "I think so. First of all you have to decide on an objective for your talk. What result do you want? For example, do you want to persuade, to entertain, motivate to action, or simply inform? Understanding the reason or motive for your presentation keeps you focused and helps you decide what content to put in or leave out."

"Okay. That's good," Jennifer commented, making notes as we went along.

"Second. You have to know what you are talking about. Do your homework or research. Don't guess or try to fudge your way through. Really effective speeches call for honesty and openness. I found out just how important that is in teaching children. Children are great at picking up on unconscious signals you give when you are not being straight with them. Kids can be a deadly audience. I suppose, for me, that's what makes it a challenge to teach."

"Maybe I should give my speech to your class for practice," Jennifer joked.

"Sure. Why not, if you dare," Susan said with a challenging grin.

I added, "Susan is right. Knowledge and honesty build your credibility which means that your audience will be predisposed to listen to you and believe you."

"That's all I can think of, Mom," Susan shrugged.

"That's okay. Those are two important points. Another consideration to add is to be courteous to the audience, which you demonstrate several ways. Be concise and keep your presentation brief. That shows respect for their time, especially in an organized business setting.

"Be organized and logical in the sequence you present ideas. Explain them simply. Don't make the audience work hard to understand you. Make sure you clarify what you say. If necessary, write it down and be sure everyone agrees on the content. Never assume everyone has the same meanings for the words you use. Clarity is the key to power in communication. It prevents misunderstandings and the wasted time and emotion they cause.

"Also, the timing and pace of your presentation

is critical. Don't rush to fill silences. People listen a whole lot slower than you can talk. Leave them time to assimilate what you say, otherwise your audience will drift off or become very irritated with you. Try to be creative and interesting in your presentation. Use humor, if you can, to keep the audience tuned in," I concluded.

"That's too much to remember all at once," Jennifer complained with a frown, looking at her notes.

"True, it does seem to be a lot," I agreed sympathetically. "But being a skillful, articulate communicator is essential to success in any career. The smartest person in the world is a failure if she can't communicate her ideas clearly to others.

"Here's where it all comes together and what makes it very easy: speak from the heart. If you know and care about your audience, and if you speak honestly, knowledgeably, and from the heart with passion, you will be an effective speaker. Passion is what it's about. Passion is what will animate you and your speech. Passion is what will evoke a stirring response in your audience," I concluded.

Jennifer looked relieved at that. Across the top of her notepad she wrote "Passion" in big letters and then drew a box around the letters. I had finally hit on something that comes naturally to her and that made her feel comfortable again. I had always enjoyed watching their high school debating teams. Susan might win the judges over with facts, figures, and the logic of her presentation, but she would lose points for her tenuous delivery. Jennifer, on the other hand, would steamroll over them with her energy and conviction. She lost points for losing her cool. One year she threw her notes at the timer for cutting her off.

I think she'll do fine. A twenty-minute presentation should give her enough time to get up a good head of steam.

"Got it!" She looked up and smiled.

"So, like any skill, you need to practice, practice, practice how you communicate with people. The more you do, the better you will get," Susan added.

"Perfect practice makes perfect." Jennifer recalled Grama's words.

"Right."

"You can practice on us," Susan offered.

"Thanks, I will."

"Do these ideas help at all?" I asked. "Yes? Good. Hopefully Grama will be feeling better next month, and I'm sure she, too, will have something to say about communication."

"You know, I'm beginning to think that you and Grama are in cahoots here, Mom." Jennifer drummed her fingers suspiciously on the table. "I'll know for sure if golden thread number ten turns out to be something about communication."

"Yeah, Mom. How much do you really know?" Susan also eyed me in playful suspicion.

"Ah, Madame Zelda knows all, sees all, and says nothing unless you cross her palm with silver." I held out my palm but they shook their heads no.

"I think we'll wait to get it straight from the source, Grama, instead of the medium!" Jennifer laughed.

Golden Thread #10

Communicate Effectively

AUGUST
You Stitched My Life Together

Lest you think otherwise, we hadn't forgotten about Robbie. He, too, had a job and would be working out west all summer and, unfortunately, he wouldn't be home. However, we wrote and telephoned him frequently.

After Jack died, Robbie spent a lot of time with Grama, just talking. Since then, he had kept up a regular correspondence with her. So he was up to date on the quilting bee. Perhaps he too was benefiting from having Grama's golden threads being spun. If he thought we were all crackers he kept it to himself.

Today we carried a package he sent to "The Four Women of Ancient Wisdom, Holders of the

Sacred Thimble, and Queen Bees of Success!" Fortunately it was a large box and he had lots of room on the label.

Naturally, we saved it for our visit with Grama and when we opened it we found four ceramic mugs, individually tagged, one for each of us. The card enclosed said: "Happy unbirthday to my favorite women. I found these in a craft shop and couldn't resist sending them. Love, Rob."

Each mug appropriately had a colorful quilt design on it and a caption.

Jennifer read hers first. It said, "Quilting Forever, Housework Whenever!"

"He must have seen pictures of your room lately," I teased her. We all know she isn't the neatest person in the world. She also likes to think of herself as a modern feminist, and of course true feminists hate housework. I keep telling her just about everyone hates housework.

Susan read her mug. "The one who dies with the most fabric wins!" Robbie had pegged her accurately. She is a packrat, worse, a sentimental packrat. She saves everything.

We all know dressmakers are packrats, and quilters are the worst. However, as Grama likes to remind us, a person who sews just makes scraps, whereas quilters use them. Out of the rejected scraps, a quilter can make a work of art, using only her creativity and inner vision to "add value" and give brand-new meaning and purpose.

Back to the mugs. It's a good thing that the men who know us best also love us. Otherwise, who knew what mine might say. I laughed as I read it. "Quilters don't do buttons." That's an inside joke, I should explain. When Robbie was home for Christmas, although he did some not-too-subtle hinting, he never did manage to have missing buttons replaced on two of his shirts. I teased him at the time to "get a girlfriend out west, or don't your 'modern' women do buttons?" He was having the last laugh.

Don't worry, he was taught to sew buttons on himself. He just didn't want to. Isn't that what mothers are for? Instead of putting wayward young men in the army for a while to straighten them out, I think every young man should be given a job as a mother for a year. Tougher than any bootcamp. I'm kidding, of course.

Grama's mug had a quilted heart design on it and it read, "Thanks, Grandma, You Stitched My Life Together."

Grama went all soft at the sentiment. "What a nice kid," she sighed. Even frequent letters couldn't substitute for a real visit. She was obviously missing him too.

"That's sweet." Susan hugged Grama as she read the mug. "Grama, that could be from any of us."

"You are so wise, Grama. You helped us all," Jennifer refrained. "How did you get to be so wise?"

"I just got old! Funny thing, you know, I said the same things forty years ago when I was your mother's age and nobody would listen," she twinkled. "Now I'm old so everyone listens. Maybe people think I will say something really brilliant before I die. Go figure." She shrugged.

"Thanks, Grama, maybe there's hope for me yet." I laughed.

"Since we received this 'communication' from Robbie let's talk today about communication. Because it, too, is a golden thread—number ten."

"Aha! I knew it!" Jennifer exclaimed triumphantly.

"Yes, Jen, I understand from your mother that you made a presentation at work and that already gave you three an opportunity to discuss communication from a technical how-to point of view. Have you talked about the message you are communicating?" Grama asked. The girls shook their heads.

"I thought we would leave that for you to cover, Grama," I deferred.

"So, again you have a success how but not a success what," she observed as she settled back into the cushions on the sofa. "Well, you know, what you communicate is a lot more important than how you communicate it. For most people 'talk is cheap.' It's just a lot of personality stuff, some flash and dazzle with no substance. When people think of effective speakers, they think of fast-talking con men out to trick them. That's because the message side of successful dialogue takes a lot more thought and consideration. Yet it's also more satisfying because that is where you truly connect with people. It's one of the most important aspects of interpersonal relationships."

"So, Grama, I guess you disagree with Marshall McLuhan who said 'the medium is the message,'" Jennifer observed.

Does any student get out of college without hearing that famous expression, I wondered. I thought it was only our generation that quoted the pop guru.

"What he said may be true—unfortunately. If television is the 'medium' of today, there are people out there making a lot of noise but not saying much. Or saying things that they haven't thought through carefully. For them it doesn't seem to matter what they say as long as they look good while saying it."

"So like Shakespeare said, we should 'shoot the messenger,'" Jennifer quipped.

"I think he said *don't* shoot the messenger," Susan corrected.

"He probably meant to say shoot the hecklers if they don't stop fooling around and interrupting." I glared at them.

"Sorry, Grama," Jennifer apologized and Grama waved "that's okay" to her.

"In any case, the point about communicating is that before you can get your message across to anyone about anything significant you have to establish a meaningful dialogue, meaningful to the other person, that is. Building an effective dialogue requires three things: empathetic listening, caring, and a willingness to share yourself with others.

"First, empathetic listening means you focus your attention on the other person, in a nonjudgmental way, to absorb not only the content of what they say, but also their feelings at the time. It can be tough to really hear someone, because we naturally tend to filter what we hear through our own reality and reinterpret what someone else says to fit our own experiences. Yet if you don't understand and deal with the true emotions of the other person, which is their reality, you don't really communicate."

"Like Mom told us, 'seek first to understand, and then seek to be understood,'" Susan volunteered.

"Right. Next you must communicate that you care. One of the simplest ways you can do this is by asking questions. Questions show that you are interested in the other person, interested to learn about them—that you value them. Questions may prompt people to reveal information or feelings that they would have been too shy to mention, or thought unimportant. And of course, you must listen to their answers, listen attentively."

"Isn't that being nosy?" Jennifer asked. "What about their privacy?"

"If someone doesn't want to answer, they don't have to, and won't, right, Grama?" Susan suggested.

"Right. Some people think asking questions is invasive, or manipulative. I disagree—as long as you are sincerely interested, and more important, as long as you are also willing to share yourself and give an honest response."

I spoke up here saying, "There is a wonderful kind of power in sharing. Not a power of control, but a power of connection to another human being. A true communion. It's one of those traits that I talked about a long time ago where women seem to have an advantage, either by our nature or by the encouragement and training we receive."

"It's true, Mom," Jennifer put in. "I find women will more often share information and be supportive of each other than men will. I sometimes wonder what these guys are afraid of?"

"Right. And like the women at the quilt show you took us to, Grama, they were complete strangers yet they opened up to us and were so friendly," Susan added.

I spoke again saying, "You certainly can't 'fake it until you make it' where caring is concerned. If it isn't sincere, it isn't real and people will know. I once worked with a woman who was always asking questions and probing people. It was as though she was studying a bug under a microscope. You didn't get the feeling that she cared at all about you or tried to understand you. She just wanted to use the information."

"So, asking questions isn't manipulative as long as you have the right intentions behind them," Jennifer said. "Okay, but what if you care and are open with someone else and they do use the information against you? Boy, I see that all the time around the office. You know, the old 'smile in your face and stab you in the back' routine."

"If you have given information about yourself freely and openly, how can it hurt you? People are usually afraid that their secrets will be found out. But if you willingly talk about yourself, no one can find you out. The way I see it, the only way to be truly invulnerable is to be vulnerable. In other words, be open," Grama answered.

"The oak and the willow," Jennifer nodded.

"Right," Grama nodded.

"What's that?" Susan frowned.

Jennifer explained. "You know the story. Although the oak is sturdy, it's also unyielding and in a strong wind it will break. On the other hand, the willow is soft and apparently weak but even in a hurricane it can bend and therefore survive because it is flexible. Its vulnerability actually makes it invulnerable. So, openness is a vulnerability, but if it's my choice, then it's a solid defense."

"I get it," Susan nodded. "Like no one can laugh at you if you are laughing at yourself."

"Right. To go back to the point," Grama redirected them. "Ask yourself this: Do you want to play the office politics game the way others do?"

"No, but if I don't . . ." Jennifer trailed off.

"Okay, so then what's the worst thing that could happen to you? You get fired? Is that worse than losing yourself? Losing your self-respect? You can always find another job. Where can you find another you?

"What we're really talking about here is integrity—which is exactly the message we were leading up to. Living with integrity means knowing what your most important values are and consistently applying them throughout your life. This may be the hardest thing you ever do. That's why I make it the eleventh golden thread and not the first. I could have told you straight out months ago, as the first golden thread for success, to Live with Integrity. Except that all the work you did building your character must come first.

"We started slow and easy for a reason. Do you remember the sampler style quilts you've seen in the magazines where each quilt block of the design has a different pattern on it?" Jennifer and Susan both nodded yes. "Well, each block is different for a reason. Each block is designed to teach the quilter a distinct and increasingly difficult lesson. When she has finished it, she has learned every quilting technique that she can then use to make any style quilt she chooses. In the same way, that's why each golden thread worked on a different block, or quality, of your character separately. Only now are you ready to stitch it all together."

"I get it," Susan said. "Every lesson builds on the previous one."

"Right. You develop who you are as a person step by step, as you make those first choices about yourself. Who is it you want to be in life? What qualities—like trustworthiness, self-discipline, confidence—do you admire in others and aspire to yourself? What values do you intend to live by? Honesty, equality, and respect may be some of those.

"Remember how the first six golden threads created inner character traits? Making and keeping commitments led to trust. Working through a plan made you self-disciplined. Quality work gave you self-esteem. Responsibility allowed you to have choices and therefore independence and maturity. In order to learn you had to stay flexible and have courage. It made you self-confident.

"The rest of the golden threads are about how you relate to people and the impact you have on the world around you. Cooperation taught you how to work effectively with people and be a team player. Contribution balanced your selfish pursuits with selflessness. And knowing you were able to persevere through the tough times enabled you to complete your destiny. Communicating effectively allowed you to connect meaningfully with people.

"Then as you began to live those qualities each day, you started to see how those choices worked successfully for you. You see, life is a testing ground for your values. Once you know what kind of person you want to be, you make this additional, conscious choice to live with integrity. Your personal integrity is that overriding quality of character that demands you hold on to those values and consistently apply them in your life.

"The choice itself seems easy. We like to think that every good person wants to live with integrity. But that can be harder than you expect because your integrity will be challenged continually, by people and situations. It isn't easy. You may be forced to make some tough, painful decisions. And it can sometimes seem that the bad guy wins while the good guy loses. There are people who will try to sabotage you for being a person who does the right thing. Either consciously or subconsciously they may envy your integrity or feel guilty because they haven't made the same right choices for themselves.

"Business is just one example where your integrity can be challenged. Unfortunately, it also happens in personal relationships. A friend or lover may try to persuade you to do things that are contrary to your values. You may feel a strong impulse to compromise your values in order to preserve harmony in the relationship or to preserve your job. But always remember, you can find another job, friend, or lover. Where can you find another you?

"Some kind of loss may be the short-term cost of having integrity, but what is the alternative?" Grama continued. "As a wise man said, 'It profit not a man to lose his soul for all the world.'"

I nodded, "That was Sir Thomas More after he'd been betrayed for his principles."

Jennifer paused and then reflected this new insight back to us. "Now I understand what you were saying about the price you may have to pay for success. If your choice is to live with integrity, it could cost you in the office politics game, for example. But if integrity itself has a higher reward, of being at peace with yourself, it is worth it. Is that what it's all about, Grama? However you define success, if it doesn't ultimately lead to peace of mind, it isn't success."

Grama nodded. "That is why the tenth golden thread is: Communicate Effectively. And it leads directly into the eleventh golden thread: Live with Integrity. The most important message you can communicate with others is your values and your integrity.

"Here's where it comes back to your quilting. We've used your quilt throughout the past year as a metaphor for your life. I like to compare the eleventh golden thread, integrity, to the final and all-important quilting stitches that hold the whole quilt together and give it definition as a unique thing. You see, a quilt is a quilt is a quilt. It's not a layered blanket, and it's not a padded sheet. It is a quilt. No matter what outward personality the surface pattern on the quilt exhibits, no matter how successful or clever the block designs may be, it is the subtle quilting stitches that define its essence, its quiltness.

"You've seen how sometimes the quilting thread is almost invisible against the patterned fabrics. But if you hold it to the light, hold it up for examination, the quilting is revealed in the depth of texture and integrity it gives to the whole. The attention and uncompromising care given to the quilting is what validates the quilt.

"Likewise, in your life you must know who you are and communicate who you are through your words and actions. Live with integrity as your highest ideal so that when your life is held up for examination you won't be found wanting."

In the car on the drive home there wasn't a lot of discussion about Grama's latest golden threads. Jennifer and Susan both appeared to be deep in concentration.

As we neared home, Jennifer finally said, "Golden threads ten and eleven: Communicate Effectively; Live with Integrity. Wow, this is serious stuff, Mom. My brain is starting to hurt!"

I waited to reply.

"But it's all so important, Jen," Susan said quietly.

"I know it is, but we still have one more golden thread to go. I can't imagine how tough that one's going to be. I'll bet Grama kept a real doozie for the last!"

"I'm glad you girls are thinking seriously about this. What Grama said this month is perhaps the most important message of all. That you have to live with integrity or lose the best and most important part of who you are. And like Grama said, 'Where can you find another you?'"

GOLDEN THREAD #11

Live with Integrity

SEPTEMBER
Celebrate Life

*I*t was a quiet drive to Clareville today. Everyone was consumed in her own thoughts. Grama has been very ill and the doctors tell us she may not be with us much longer. It seemed sudden, but at eighty-five not surprising. Perhaps we should have seen it coming. Would we have done anything differently?

The girls are upset. To be so young and to be reminded again that life doesn't go on forever, that cherished loved ones aren't immortal and won't be there forever, whenever we need their wisdom and comfort.

Susan sat with her arms clutched around her quilt bag just the way she held her teddy bear when she was a sad baby, unconsciously stroking the soft material.

"I wish we lived closer to Grama. We could have visited her more. We should have," Jennifer pined.

I wish. We could have. We should have. Ah, Jen. Would we have? To live a life with no regrets.

I squeezed her hand. "It's okay, Sweetie, Grama knows we all love her. Love is not always being right there with someone all the time. The love goes on when you're not with them and when you're not even thinking of them. Grama is so proud of you guys. She gets a big kick out of seeing her little birdies fly free. In the meantime, let's try to make it peaceful for her. All right? The greatest gift of love you can give her right now is not to have her see you unhappy. Okay?"

Two quiet, sad faces looked at me. A quick exchanged glance at each other. Two faint but determined nods. And three deep breaths. Yes, we can do this. Let's go.

Jennifer led the way. We can always count on her to have courage, to be noisy and funny, and to cover her bad feelings with a smile. For someone so boisterous and opinionated, surprisingly she can be compassionate and loving of others. It gives her strength and grace beyond her years.

"Hi, Yoda-Grama," she called out cheerfully. "Look what we brought. Bet you thought we weren't ever going to finish! Sometimes even I didn't think we would," she joked as she pulled out her quilt. "*Voilà!*" She unfurled her quilt gently over the hospital bed. Grama was in the extended-care section of the residence where she could receive more immediate medical attention.

"Today we celebrate!" I hugged Grama. "The ordeal is over," I pretended to whisper to her.

"Mine's done too, Grama," Susan said more quietly and squeezed in a hug. She draped her quilt over a chair beside the bed where Grama could see.

"This is truly wonderful," Grama exclaimed softly as she examined the finished work. "I am so proud of you. For a first effort, you have both made a beautiful top-quality quilt."

"And we owe it all to you, Grama," Jennifer said.

"All," I emphasized as I leaned over to kiss her, "and it was worth it."

"But not so fast," Grama interrupted, shaking her finger at us. "You have one more task to do. Remember, you have to date and sign your quilts. Here, I've been waiting to give you these. I made signature labels for you and here is my waterproof marker. You write out your labels and sew them neatly to the back of your quilts. Then you are finished." Her frail hand shook as she handed over the pens.

The girls were quick and eager to comply. As

they nimbly slipstitched their labels on, I marveled at how easily and nonchalantly they now worked. Their new dexterity gave maturity and confidence to their stitches.

Grama and I exchanged smiles. She nodded and continued, "This is the last and most important part. It's an important tradition to sign your quilt. In other words, take credit for your work. Always do work that you are proud to put your name on. That's an excellent motivator. Knowing you will sign your name to your work is a good way to make sure that you always do your best."

"Fewer lemons would roll off the new car assembly lines if everyone who worked on each car had to sign their name to the bumper," Jennifer pointed out. We laughed at her example.

"Right," Grama agreed. "And, of course, quality work should always be honored and celebrated."

"By that token," Susan added, "every auto worker should be given good points for every car that isn't a lemon."

Grama chuckled.

"And so, the last and twelfth golden thread is: Celebrate Life! Celebrate your accomplishments and feel proud of yourself. That will motivate you to keep doing things, the right things. You are both unique and valuable women and you have so much to give. Stand up and take your place in the big world out there. Listen to your Grama. She knows.

"Make sure the last thing you do is celebrate, your work and your life. Life is too short not to be happy and have fun.

"There, you finally have all the twelve golden threads. I hope they help you. So, like Mr. Spock says, 'Live long and prosper.'" She twinkled, raising a pontifical hand in the now famous splayed-finger Vulcan blessing. "And celebrate!"

"Right on, Grama!" exclaimed Jennifer.

"Boy, are we glad to hear that, Grama. We thought number twelve was going to be a real tough one, but this is one we can definitely handle." Susan laughed and they both hugged Grama happily.

Twelve months had passed and twelve golden threads for success had been spun. Like a village wise-woman, Grama had passed on her life secrets, and the young women had been initiated into her ways. Graduation day was here. There was a special gleam in Grama's eye, of relief, satisfaction, and completion.

"Lock in the good times!" Jack used to say. So that is what we would do today. We would talk and reminisce on the year we had been through. We would laugh at the agonies and tease each other because that is the gentle way to laugh with someone else, with affection, while we laugh at ourselves, with forgiveness. We would applaud the breakthroughs and the growth. We would share our feelings, unguarded, because we were with women who care and listen and support.

Women do this so well.

We had brought glasses and "champagne" (a bottle of ginger ale) to toast the victory of the completed quilts. Susan shook the bottle so it splattered and fizzed when opened. We all said "Pop!" for the cork and sipped it quickly so it would tickle our noses and make us laugh. Silly, you say? Probably. Oh, well.

And we took pictures so we could remember and share the memories.

Grama tired quickly and so we couldn't stay long. Soon there would be other longer, sadder visits. I knew Grama wanted this special day to be all sunshine for Jennifer and Susan, to be a warm memory for them. A memory of completion and celebration, unclouded by sadness or pain. So I started to make clean-up, wrap-up motions.

Grama looked at me. "Would you do me a favor, honey, and go tell Mrs. Wells I would like to see her for a few minutes after you leave today? Thank you."

This was a fairly transparent ploy to make me leave the room so I did as she asked. I guessed that there were some private words for the girls that needed some space.

I was only gone a few minutes, though, and when I returned the girls were each sitting on the sides of her bed. Grama was holding their hands while they fought back tears. Jennifer held a piece of paper in her other hand which she quickly folded and put in her pocket.

Grama patted their hands. "Now, now," she soothed. "Off you go. You have a long drive ahead. Give these old bones a big hug before you leave. I am so proud of you both. Your beautiful quilts. And two beautiful talented young women. I know you are both going to do so well in life."

"We love you, Grama," they said as they hugged her again.

"I have one shot left," I said, lifting the camera. "Jen, Suz, with Grama, and the quilts," I directed and we popped the flash on the last champagne memory.

The warm communion of the day left Jennifer and Susan peaceful and close to Grama for a while, as every visit does. Yet as we drove home in the bright sunshine, a sadness washed over them that they couldn't deny.

"What did you see today?" I asked gently.

"All of a sudden Grama seems so frail. She never used to look so small and old," Jennifer remarked softly.

"A frail old lady we love who is slipping away from us," Susan added quietly.

"Frail in body, yes. But frail in spirit, never. Girls, I'm not going to tell you not to be sad. But don't be upset for Grama. Don't regret not doing more. There is no unfinished business in your relationship with Grama. She knows you love her.

"That's what I saw today. A great deal of love. And I am so proud of you both. You know, Grama is very pleased you let her teach you to make a quilt, and more important, her golden threads for success. You gave her a great gift of love simply by listening to her. You gave her the satisfaction, at the end of a long life, of knowing that she was able to pass on her knowledge and her wisdom to another generation. You let her complete her life. You let her fulfill a purpose. By treasuring her quilts and valuing her golden threads you have given her immortality—she will live on in the work of her skilled hands and in her words of wisdom.

"You know, at the beginning of your quilt odyssey we identified Grama as a role model, for her expertise in quilting. And, as you quickly found out, she has lots to say about life. Her words and her golden threads are only part of the lesson. Look at her life itself. There are subtle lessons there also. She may be telling you things by example that you are not even aware of."

"Like what, Mom?" Susan asked.

"Well, has Grama ever given you the feeling that she regrets anything in her life? No? Of course not. It isn't enough to say she has lived a good long life. She lived a whole life. Her life is an example.

"Grama has always been in harmony with herself and done what's right for her. And she has always done what she ultimately knew was right. When congruency and integrity meet, you have true peace of mind. Grama has that. As you pointed out one time, that is the ultimate success, girls, to have peace of mind."

Jennifer and Susan nodded in thoughtful silence and we drove the rest of the way home in a lighter melancholy.

Golden Thread #12

Celebrate Life

OCTOBER

Fallen Leaves

So now this is where I have to take over for Grama. Our beloved Grama.

Grama died three days ago.

There are no words to describe the ache we all feel.

Forgive me that I can only leave the rest of the page blank with just the sound of my heart beating in the emptiness.

November
A Pattern Changes

The quilts are finished and without the regular trips to visit Grama we are all feeling lost. Not only for the special person we miss but also because a pattern in our lives has been changed forever, and the readjusting will take time.

In talking about Grama these last weeks, Jennifer and Susan have realized that the poignant irony of Grama's death is that although her wisdom, humor, and love was once only a telephone call away, now they have internalized Grama's golden threads as part of their character. So there is no spiritual distance at all between them. That has helped them to acceptance and peace of mind.

This is a time for healing. A time for remembrance and reflection.

DECEMBER
Everything with Love

We made several trips to Clareville in the last three months. There were many details to wrap up, even for an old soul who lived simply. Today was a special, happier trip, though. The residence director, Mrs. Wells, called us a few days ago and told us that Grama's friends wanted to give back to us all of her quilts she had made while she lived there. No ingratitude intended, but a gesture to give her love back to us. A gift of love in the season of giving.

Jennifer and Susan were overwhelmed at the sight of over twenty quilts, cleaned and neatly folded on Mrs. Wells's desk. A tower of soft folds and a riot of colors kaleidoscoping into each other.

DECEMBER: EVERYTHING WITH LOVE

"Oh, Jen, they're so beautiful," whispered Susan as she gingerly picked up the top one and held it to her cheek in automatic childlike soothing action.

"This is wonderful," Jennifer replied brightly, taking the next one and letting the folds open freely, the quilt flowing from her arms.

"Can we go thank everyone?" Susan asked, looking up at me.

"I think that would be a very gracious thing to do," I replied, taking a third quilt from the pile.

Guided by Mrs. Wells, we made our way slowly from room to room, in some cases simultaneously saying first hellos and last good-byes to the strangers who had all been Grama's friends. The director introduced us as we went and told us bits of information about each resident. A blur of names and wrinkled faces and infirm hands. Many, many smiles.

On the way back to Mrs. Wells's office, as we passed through the lounge, she pointed out, "Here are Mrs. Shaw and Mr. Fulton." She introduced us as we approached two people seated in wheelchairs.

"Henry, these are Alice's girls, her granddaughters Jennifer and Susan," she spoke louder with each word. "They've come to say hello!"

"Bellow? I'm not bellowing, you are!" he said grumpily.

"We want to thank you," I started but Susan interrupted.

"I remember you, Mr. Fulton. Your quilt is the

extra-soft one because you have trouble with your skin," Susan tried loudly.

"Thin? I've always been thin," he replied with a dismissing gesture. "Who did you say you are?"

The girls laughed gently. "I'm Jennifer. This is Susan. We're granddaughters of Alice Myers."

"Alice? She's dead!" he yelled back. "Gone! Doesn't live here now. I already gave back the quilt she made me. Looked just like yours there," he pointed at me. "Gave it to her granddaughter. Well, you never know about girls. Mebbe she don't want it. If not, then she can give it back to me."

"Oh, Henry, just go on now!" yelled Mrs. Shaw in the chair beside him. "He's deaf as a doorknob." She shook her head at the girls. "Never mind him," she continued and, taking Jennifer's and Susan's hands firmly in hers, she looked at each of them intently and said, "Your Grama did everything with love." She shook their hands fiercely up and down as if to make the thought stick, that it was important to remember. "Everything with love," she repeated emphatically. She squeezed their hands and let them go, waving them away.

Susan echoed softly to Jennifer as we continued down the hall, "Grama did everything with love."

Jennifer nodded. "Do everything with love. That's the last lesson, Suzie. If there are golden threads, then there must be a golden needle. Do everything with love is the golden needle Grama used to stitch all her golden threads through life," she said, putting her arm around Susan's shoulder.

"She had so much more to tell us," Susan pined sadly.

"No, I think she said it all. It all comes down to love. Do everything with love," Jennifer reassured Susan.

I nodded to myself as I followed behind them. Grama could still speak to the girls. We are immortal as long as we live on in people's memories.

Back home, we hurried to unpack the car so we could explore our treasures one by one.

"Look, Mom," Susan drew my attention to something we hadn't noticed before. "There's a note pinned to this quilt."

"What does it say?" I asked putting down another bundle.

"It's a list. There's names and dates." She looked puzzled.

"Here's another one, on this quilt," said Jennifer, holding up a corner with one hand, flipping through the rest of the pile with the other. They looked at each other. Every quilt had a note pinned carefully to the back of one corner.

"These are all the people who had the quilt," said Jennifer, suddenly inspired. "Look. 'Mr. King, died February 18, 1987.' 'Mr. Charbonneau, died June 27, 1989.' 'Mrs. Epstein, no date.'"

"Because she's still alive," Susan jumped in. "We

met her. She was wearing that funny fox fur collar, remember. She must have had this quilt last."

"This is weird," said Jennifer. "Look at this," she said finding another note. "This one goes back twenty years. It must have been one of the first quilts Grama made there. Look at all the names."

"Now, don't unpin them," I warned. "Let's not get the notes all mixed up."

"This is amazing. All these people. Wow!" Susan enthused, picking up one after another and finding the note on each. "All these people," she repeated in amazement.

From a small personal quilting hobby and a love of people, Grama had unwittingly touched many lives over the years. Like drops in a bucket, each small act of love had added up to more than a full measure.

"Who did all this?" Jennifer wondered aloud.

"Probably the director, Mrs. Wells. She's worked at the home for almost twenty years. She probably remembers all these people herself," I offered. "It was very kind of her to go to this effort for us." I joined the girls in their amazement and pleasure.

"It must have been quite a job to track down the history of each quilt," Susan observed. "We should write and thank her," she suggested and we nodded agreement.

Over the days that followed, we wallowed in

quilts. To see the colors, sometimes bright and gaudy, other times somber and melancholy. We wondered aloud what Grama had been thinking at the time, what kind of mood she had been in while she was working on each quilt. Questions we never thought to ask when she was alive. Aren't there always questions we forget to ask.

Sometimes the stitching was smooth, even, and confident. Sometimes it was a little shaky. Had she been ill at those times in her life? Or just tired and inattentive? She told us once that a quilt is a self-portrait of the person who made it. If that is true, then quilting can also be a biography of the quilter, if we are perceptive enough to read the subtle clues. There could be no better story of Grama's life than the body of work she left behind.

Searching through her books and magazines we found the traditional names for the quilt designs and laughed at the funny-sounding names like Turkey Tracks, Monkey Wrench, and Kitten in the Corner. Names from the pioneer women who were her spiritual grandmothers. We discovered the quilt names, and naming them, they became ours.

It had never occurred to me before that a quilter puts her own emotions into her work, that each quilt could be an expression of her joy, or her deep sorrow. Or that even behind a deceptively pretty and elegant quilt pattern could be a heart healing itself through creativity and love. We were sad when we realized that the beautiful yet somber navy, gray and, white quilt called Storm at Sea was made the year after Jack died. We renamed it Daddy's Quilt and the girls put it on my bed.

Jennifer and Susan decided to catalog the quilts so I bought them a photo album. We photographed each quilt, labeled the photo and placed it in the book next to the note that had been pinned to it.

Freed from the concern of damaging or confusing the identifying notes, now we could really enjoy Grama's quilts. We piled them on our beds, draped them on our chairs and hung each in rotation on the wall over the living room sofa.

One evening, after we had more or less returned to our normal routines, Jennifer said pensively, "You know, Mom, we really should do something with Grama's quilts."

"Like what?" I asked.

"I don't know." She hesitated. "I feel sort of bad that we have them all here. Grama made them for other people to enjoy. You know, at the residence. People who needed them."

"You don't want to give them back, do you?" Susan asked in alarm, putting down the book she was reading.

"Well no, of course not. I mean I feel we should give them back but I don't want to. I feel so selfish. Does that make any sense?" she asked me.

"Of course it does," I assured her. "Is there any

other way that you could still keep the quilts but that other people could enjoy them too?"

"Loan them out to the old folks, I guess." She shrugged weakly.

"What about putting them in a quilt show?" Susan suggested. "Do you think a show would take Grama's quilts, Mom?"

"Well, it's possible," I replied.

"Wait a minute. Why don't we make our own show? We could do that, couldn't we, Mom," Jennifer declared.

"Sure," I started to say, "But . . ."

"You bet we can, Jen," Susan said emphatically, immediately catching Jennifer's inspiration and enthusiasm. "That's a great idea. What a terrific way to let other people see and enjoy Grama's quilts. After all, Grama taught us everything we need to know to be successful at anything! Remember, the golden threads!"

"Right on! What's the first golden thread? Make a Commitment!" Jennifer asked and answered her own question.

"Okay. I will if you will," Susan promised. "How about you, Mom?"

"Glad you remembered I'm here," I kidded.

"Sorry, Mom. But, Suz, I think if we do this, we should do it ourselves, right? You understand, Mom, don't you?" Jennifer asked, hoping I wouldn't be offended at being excluded.

"Of course I do. But can I listen in?" I replied.

"Sure," she nodded. "So, Susan, now we're committed. Or should be." Susan laughed.

"Next we imagine the outcome by seeing in our mind's eye all Grama's quilts on display and lots of people coming to admire them. Then we find a role model, an expert, and do what they do," Jennifer recalled.

"The women who organized the quilt show that we saw last summer might advise us or be able to suggest someone who can," Susan suggested. "That's what you called mentoring, isn't it, Mom?"

I nodded yes.

"Good idea. Now golden thread number two is Set a Goal. That would mean we describe exactly what we want to do and set a date for it," Jennifer recalled. "Then golden thread number three. We need a plan. We have to write it down, and remember all the S–T–E–P–S," Jennifer continued. "Keep it simple. Have a time frame for each item of action to be finished. Keep it efficient by balancing time against accuracy."

"We have to prioritize the plan, by what's most important first, and how urgent it is. Do first things first," Susan finished. "And start now, don't forget," she added.

"Next. We have to take responsibility—golden thread number four—and be flexible if something goes wrong." Jennifer was nodding her head yes while remembering the Hobbes incident and smiling. It had been a particularly significant life lesson for her.

"Golden thread number five is Always Do Quality Work. Let's face it, we can make this the best quilt show ever!" exclaimed Susan confidently. She continued, "And Grama's golden thread number six is to learn from our mistakes as we make them and keep going. I almost forgot our postgraduate lesson. We have to add zest by stretching ourselves, but since we've never made a quilt show happen before, this whole thing is definitely out of our comfort zones!" She was remembering her own former lack of self-confidence.

"What else?" Jennifer was thinking. "We covered all the inner work, commitment, goals, planning, responsibility, quality work, and learning."

"What about cooperation?" I suggested.

"Hey, Mom. Come on now. We're sisters! When do we ever not cooperate?" Jennifer put her arm over Susan's shoulder and they laughed.

"Of course. Silly me!" I mocked back.

"Mom's right. Golden thread number seven is Cooperate. This really is a win-win situation," Susan observed. "We get to keep the quilts and other people get to enjoy them too. Maybe seeing Grama's beautiful quilts will make a difference in people's lives or even inspire them to make a quilt."

Jennifer nodded. "Maybe we could charge admission and give the money to charity or to the seniors' residence in Clareville," she suggested as her enthusiasm gathered speed, and their ideas continued to tumble out. It was like watching water sizzle on a hot griddle.

"What a great idea. Grama would like that. Contribute to society, make a difference in people's lives. Golden thread number eight." Susan definitely supported the idea.

"If we become discouraged or unmotivated, or catch the p-moan-ia bug, we know how to cope: take Grama's p-medicine of patience, perfection, perseverance, persistence, and pride." Jennifer recalled golden thread number nine. "We'll also remember to 'get out around positive people,' like the other quilters Grama introduced us to."

Susan again picked up the theme. "Grama's golden threads numbers ten and eleven. Communicate integrity is the biggest challenge of all and the most important. But like Grama said, symbolically quilting is all about communicating integrity. So putting on a quilt show is really demonstrating, or in other words communicating, what quilting, and therefore integrity, is all about. Fortunately, the last, celebrate, is the easiest. We can certainly make our quilt show a joyful celebration. After all, celebrating Grama's life is what it would be all about."

"You bet." Jennifer nodded and put out her hand, and they shook hands to seal the agreement. "Let's do it."

"And let's not forget, do everything with love," Jennifer reminded them, and Susan nodded. They were quiet for a moment remembering Grama.

"What should we call the show, Jen?" Susan asked, bringing them back to the matter at hand.

"I don't know. Let's see. How about 'A Celebration of Quilts'?" she offered. "Or, 'A Life in Quilts'?"

"Nah. It's been done before. I saw it in one of Grama's magazines," Susan countered.

"How about, 'Grama's Quilts: Yesterday and Today'?"

"Um. 'Quilts: A Way of Life'?"

"I've got it: 'Grama's Quilts: A Way of Life'?"

"No. It should be 'Grandmother's Quilts.'"

"Right. And, 'A Woman's Way of Life.'"

"That's it," they chorused. "Grandmother's Quilts—A Woman's Way of Life."

GRAMA'S GOLDEN NEEDLE
Do Everything with Love

SPRING

Full Circle

*J*t's April again. Spring is breaking out everywhere. Robbie will be home soon. He made excellent marks again this year at college. This summer he decided he wanted to work closer to home, in order to catch up on some home cooking no doubt.

Jennifer was promoted last week to Customer Service Assistant Manager. She is talking about moving into her own apartment. I've been hearing a lot about one particular fellow named Jim, so I guess it's time we had him over to a family dinner for inspection and close order drill.

Susan is doing extremely well at college, studying to become a teacher. In her practice-teaching weeks, one principal was so impressed with her maturity and confidence, he suggested she apply for a summer school job with them, and indicated he would consider her for a full-time position when she graduates.

So I'm a happy and proud Momma.

Yes, their quilt show opened last Saturday. They decided to hold it at the Quilt Inn, a hotel in Clareville, Grama's hometown, where people would know and remember her. The girls enlisted the local quilt guild to help. There they found many talented, experienced women and made new friends. The guild members were so intrigued with the idea and so impressed with Jennifer and Susan that many volunteered their time and lots of helpful advice for organizing their show. The local newspaper ran free ads and did a color piece on it.

Funny how word travels through that network of women who talk, and share, and care. That connectedness, which many men haven't come to understand and too many dismiss as just women gossiping.

When news spread of the show dedicated to Alice Myers and her quilts, strangers from all over started to write us. Grama's old friends, with memories. Young relatives of the people at the home in Clareville, with thanks. All their contributions were added to the show. A dozen more quilts were generously sent to be displayed, and then to be kept by the girls.

We reach out to touch and we never know how or when the touch will be returned.

One of Grama's quilts came just last week. Old and worn and faded and much-used, as a well-loved quilt should be. It was barely recognizable. The note said, "I'm sorry this quilt is in such bad shape. I've washed it many times. My aunt gave it to me I can't remember how many years ago. She told me stories about your grandmother and living on the farm. She always said Alice was the kindest person she ever knew."

Not a bad way to be remembered, I thought. The kindest person she ever knew. A suitable legacy for a successful life. Grama would have been pleased, I'm sure.

I hope to be so fortunately labeled when I'm gone. I want to be like one of Grama's quilts—faded, well washed, frayed with good use, and well loved. With a story attached that will be handed on in the hearts of others.

Early Saturday morning before their quilt show opened Jennifer and Susan took me on a VIP tour, my first glimpse of the culmination of all their efforts.

At the front of the hall, the girls had an enlargement of the last photo of Grama, with them and their quilts. Beside it they wrote the story of how Grama, their beloved Yoda-Grama, taught them her twelve golden threads—how to live and build their character and to be successful in life. They added their own insight, that the golden needle, Do Everything with Love, stitched it all together.

Jennifer and Susan had taken Grama's last,

unfinished quilt and secretly finished the quilting and the binding. "It's a surprise. You'll see it at the show," they told me when I pried. The sewing room had been "action central" and off limits to me, and Hobbes, for months. And there at the front door was Grama's last appliqué quilt. Hearts and Roses. So distinctively Grama. There were hearts cut from Jack's old shirt. There were roses cut from dresses the girls had worn years ago. I hadn't noticed before that there were even some new scraps from Jennifer and Susan's quilts worked into the pattern, along with dozens of other fabrics, all remnants from a lifetime, all holding favorite memories. Whoever said "God gave us memory so we would have roses in December," must have known Grama.

"Look, Jen," I pointed, "there's the material from the sunsuit Grama made for your third birthday. You were wearing it in the photos taken the summer we spent at Graham Lake. I remember you making mudpies—for the barbecue! And, Susan, there's material from your first fancy dress for the teen dance. Ever wonder what happened to that boy, Roger, that you went with?"

"Oh, yeah. I never noticed it before." She smiled at her own memories.

Each of us would look at Grama's quilt through the filter of our personal memories and see different things.

You might know Grama would weave all those

memories into her last quilt. This is a quilt full of family history, of shared times, love, and laughter. I was glad it was finished and the girls had it. This way Grama could continue to talk with us and reminisce. Grama would always be a part of Jennifer and Susan. And Robbie. And me.

This is true immortality. No one lives for an eternity but everyone can have an everlasting impact. We live on in the people and the legacy we leave behind.

"Oh, girls, this is so beautiful!" I exclaimed as we stood together with my arms around their waists, admiring her masterpiece. I hugged them as I looked over the detailed appliqué and fine quilting stitches, Grama's, Jennifer's, and Susan's, all intertwined. Threads connecting the generations.

"It's for you, Mom," Jennifer squeezed me back.

"Grama wanted you to have this quilt," Susan confirmed.

"She was making it for you," Jennifer nodded.

"How do you know that?" I queried with tears starting.

"She told us, Mom," Jennifer gently explained. "When we saw her in September. Remember when she asked you to talk to Mrs. Wells?"

"That was just to make you leave the room," Susan expanded. I nodded remembering the day.

"She told us when you left. Read the signature plate on the back, Mom. Grama had written out what she wanted us to put on it for her," Jennifer went on. "She knew she wasn't going to be able to finish it so she asked us to carry on for her."

Yes, these girls would carry on for Grama. They would continue to learn and grow. They would use their experiences to become wise, and in their turn they would hand on the tradition, and their wisdom, to other young women. Life would come full circle and continue.

"We embroidered it on. By hand, of course," Susan said proudly.

"We used some shiny gold thread we found in a craft shop," Jennifer pointed out. "We thought Grama would like that."

I turned back the bottom right-hand corner and there was the neatly lettered dedication in golden thread.

To Angela,
Given with Love unending
For Love given unmeasured
Alice Myers, 1905-1990
Completed by her granddaughters,
Jennifer and Susan

GRAMA'S GOLDEN NEEDLE
Do Everything with Love

GRAMA'S TWELVE GOLDEN THREADS
Make a Commitment

Set a Goal

Plan Your Work and Work Your Plan

Always Do Quality Work

Take Responsibility and Be Response-able

Make Learning a Lifelong Habit

Cooperate

Contribute and Make a Difference

Persevere Through the Tough Times

Communicate Effectively

Live with Integrity

Celebrate Life

A NOTE FROM THE AUTHOR

During the twenty years I've been in business and consulting, I've read dozens of "success" books and attended countless self-improvement seminars and I have found the following recurrent problems. First, our success is often equated with money, power, and fame, with the appeal to our basic fears and greed. Second, the programs too often are a quick-fix solution based on personality tricks, rather than the development of character based on values. And third, an externally driven time-management system replaces an internally driven self-management.

I believe there is a softer, gentler message to be told. One of values and integrity and one that is closer to life, reality, and work as most women know them.

Many "how-to" or "success" programs are developed by, and are about, men—using male business, sports, or warfare models and metaphors. The sometimes gratuitous, and sometimes genuine, dissembler being a "by the way, if you are a woman, this also applies to you." I did not set out to write a stridently women's book. I like men, a lot. But I did want to write a book that uses a strong woman's metaphor. Thus from my own many hours spent quilting, thinking, and creating, came this book.

I hope someday we come up with a different word for mentoring that will reflect the way women support and nurture others—in terms of their emotional needs, rather than just factual how-to-do-the-job terms. Let me know if you hear of one.

I wish you all the best and peace of mind.

Aliske Webb